TREASURE BY DEGREES

It was then that the lady fell off her bicycle, causing Henry Pink to swerve and stop with an alacrity customarily associated with Trafalgar Square in the rush hour.

Pink glanced round at his employer. 'I never touched her, sir.'

Treasure was already out of the car, making for the tangled mound of tweed, machinery, and stout flailing legs fetched up on the verge a yard ahead of where the car had stopped. His approach was momentarily arrested by the emergence from the pile of an enormous black cat – back arched, fur raised, teeth bared – that sprang into a sentinel position before the confused mass. Treasure had never seen such a large cat. It hissed at him venemously.

'Tottle, behave.' This command had no evident effect upon the cat, and came in a rich contralto from underneath the bicycle.

Risking the feline threat, Treasure advanced upon the disentangling heap in time to assist the robust, dishevelled, and aged owner of the voice to her feet.

TREASURE BY DEGREES

David Williams

A Hamlyn *Whodunnit*

Hamlyn Paperbacks

A Hamlyn Paperback

Published by Arrow Books Limited
17-21 Conway Street, London W1P 6JD

A division of the Hutchinson Publishing Group

London Melbourne Sydney Auckland
Johannesburg and agencies
throughout the world

First published in Great Britain
by Collins (The Crime Club) 1977

Hamlyn Paperbacks edition 1983

Printed and bound in Great Britain by
Anchor Brendon Ltd, Tiptree, Essex

ISBN 0 600 20618 1

This one for Rene and Jenny

Cause

CHAPTER I

'BUT, MY DEAR chap, you must have played Funny Farms at some time in your life.' Mark Treasure, Vice-Chairman of Grenwood, Phipps & Co., merchant bankers, punctuated this remark by affecting a look of benign good humour over the gold-rimmed half-glasses. He had been cultivating this particular expression – chin down, eyebrows raised, the long, lean face still undeniably youthful under the hardly receding hairline. He doubted anyone would credit he had reached forty; he could scarcely do so himself. The glasses, recently accepted as inevitable – like the last birthday – were adapting nicely as a prop to sagacity. Vanity and middle age were also coming to terms.

The histrionics were entirely wasted upon Wilfred Jonkins, Assistant Manager of the Trust Department for the last twelve of his fifty-nine years. For his part he perceived Treasure as the promising young graduate who, despite the lack of any family connection to speak of, had been tipped to achieve great heights when he joined the bank nearly two decades earlier. This promise long since fulfilled, Jonkins's image of Treasure was unaltering and would have remained so even if his superior had appeared with a long, white beard and a hearing trumpet.

The fact remained that Wilfred Jonkins had never played Funny Farms. Further, he had never even heard of Funny Farms until the day before. Since he had no enduring corporate ambition save the attainment of pensionable age two years hence, he had no hesitation in imparting this extra intelligence to 'young' Mr Treasure.

'Well, I never,' said Treasure. 'How surprising. D'you know, I remember playing it in the nursery, before we were old enough to grasp Monopoly. Then there was Lexicon, and I suppose Scrabble came next . . . or perhaps that was much later: strange how the fashions change. But Funny Farms was always my favourite – really to quite a ripe age.' This was followed by a good-natured grunt, consciously intended to emphasize the obviously relative nature of the last remark.

'I did once play Monopoly,' volunteered Jonkins, re-calling that single experience with distaste. 'The wife and I . . . that is, bridge is more . . .'

'More in your line,' interrupted Treasure. 'Very sensible too. Tell me, how is Mrs Jonkins?' he enquired opportunely on the strength of the information that such a person existed.

'Very nicely, thank you, sir.' Jonkins displayed none of the disappointment he felt at this galling admission. He had been passively plotting the woman's destruction for years.

'Good,' said Treasure, unconscious of his innocent solecism as well as the secret criminal propensities of Jonkins, who not only looked like a churchwarden, but also was one. Treasure glanced down at the documents on his desk. 'Well, despite the lack of your personal patron-age, Funny Farms appears to have been in the top selling league of what are called board games for more than forty years. And a highly profitable operation it is too.'

'The company does make other games, sir.'

'Yes. Funny Schools, Funny Films, oh, and I see here Funny Golf – never heard of that before.' Treasure had played golf for Oxford.

'Hardly your style, sir,' Jonkins put in deferentially. 'I don't believe they earn much from the other games.'

'No, they're just spin-offs. Our research people say that Funny Farms is still the breadwinner, and Funny Farms Incorporated made twenty million dollars before tax last year – which would seem to underwrite the stability of the Funny Farms Foundation. Well, no doubt I shall hear more about that at lunch.'

'Yes, sir. The capital value of the Foundation is just

over fifteen million dollars. Most of the assets are in Funny Farms Incorporated preference and ordinary stock made over by the late Mr Hatch during his lifetime.'

'Mmm, the Foundation business is clear enough, though I must say I find the whole thing a bit eccentric. What's potentially embarrassing is the prospect of all this manna from Pennsylvania being showered on University College, Itchendever. Anyway, you think Lord Grenwood's going to feel cock-a-hoop when he hears?'

'I don't believe there's any conflict of interest, Mr Treasure,' said Jonkins earnestly. 'In any event, you should be able to contact the Chairman through the Sydney office in the next twenty-four hours. We telexed last night.'

Treasure privately wished that the Chairman of Grenwood, Phipps would spend more time tending the good works he espoused and less of it inspecting mining explorations in the Australian outback. 'See for yourself' was an excellent motto for a merchant banker but an impracticable one when it led a septuagenarian with indifferent health into making an uncomfortable expedition to antipodean fastnesses. It also made normal and necessary communication tiresomely difficult.

'I think I agree on the interest of the parties being compatible,' said Treasure slowly. 'I'm more concerned about Lord Grenwood's view on whether his pet educational establishment should house the Funny Farms Faculty of Agriculture. Are they absolutely immovable about the name?'

'I'm afraid so, sir,' answered Jonkins, shuffling through the papers he was holding in search of supporting evidence. 'If I might venture Lord Grenwood's likely reaction as Chairman of the University College Trustees, I think he will be very much in favour of acceptance. The College is seriously short of funds.'

'You mean they're damned nearly broke so it's a question of Funny Farms or . . . er . . . or founder?'

Treasure was pleased with the alliteration, and absolutely accurate in his judgement. It was the nod of affirmation from Jonkins that established his resolve to pursue the proposition before him. Even had Treasure taken a different decision it is doubtful whether that same project would have been abandoned. Grenwood's enthusiastic approval was received within the day. There were, in any case, too many other interested parties involved for Treasure later to feel that his resolve did more than precipitate subsequent events by a few hours. Nevertheless, he was too sensitive a man not to be affected by the fact that the most memorable of those events was cold-blooded murder.

It had been in the winter of 1929 that Cyrus and Amelia Hatch had sold their Pennsylvania farmstead and moved into Pittsburgh. The couple were childless, and destined to remain so. Their failure to make a living from the land and the need to cut their losses and start afresh was thus a good deal easier than it might have been with a family to feed. In addition, Cyrus Hatch had been a man of intelligence with an evidently inventive mind. A farmer by inheritance, not vocation, the Depression had acted as a spur to his ambition to abandon farming and to seek a more profitable field of endeavour. He was also an optimist.

Hatch had been to Europe to fight the Germans as a pilot in the Air Corps. Travel had broadened his mind. Hours of waiting between sorties had turned him into a skilled card player. It was this last interest that was partly to form the basis of his future fortune.

Business school lecturers of a later, more sophisticated, generation might have said that Cyrus Hatch saw a potentially profitable market gap and proceeded to fill it. Indeed, several such sages made just this claim for Cyrus though he would have regarded it as a pretentious description of what really happened. Simply, he drew up a board and rules for a game he and his wife had been playing during the long winter evenings on the farm. They had called it 'Going to Market'. They played it with the aid of a pack of cards, and counters representing sheep, cows, pigs, and chickens. It was not a complicated game but it was certainly more stimulating than checkers, a change from conventional card games, and it appealed to young and old alike.

On the gratuitous and shrewd advice of an ex-pilot friend who had started an advertising business in Pittsburgh, Hatch made two alterations to the prototype of the game. He designed a special pack of sixty cards to be used instead of an ordinary pack, and he replaced the counters with tiny lead replicas of real farm animals – thus reducing the possibility of imitation, home-made or otherwise. He also changed the name of the game to Funny Farms. The rest of the story is legend – despite its failure to have touched the consciousness of Wilfred Jonkins.

Within five years the rurally oriented game of Funny Farms had penetrated every self-respecting urban household in America. It was approved by educationalists, blessed by the thankful parents of happily occupied children, and played by Franklin D. Roosevelt, in public, at a Farmers For The New Deal Convention in Chicago. It also made Cyrus Hatch a millionaire by 1934.

By the outbreak of the Second World War subsidiary companies of Funny Farms Inc. had been established in fourteen countries. It was not until 1970 that a Russian version of the game, royalties paid, became available at the GUM department store in Moscow. The misguided bureaucrat responsible – a convinced capitalist at heart – was certain that a knowledge of the game would act as an incentive to Collectivist farmers. Thereafter Funny Farms was much played inside the Kremlin – but hardly anywhere else in the Soviet Union.

Cyrus Hatch continued to lead the business until he was well into his seventies – latterly to the considerable embarrassment of those who were doing all the work. He hovered in a state of what was euphemistically described as mild eccentricity for some time before it had to be admitted that he had become distinctly dotty. His whim for inventing impossibly complicated board games was easy to humour, though it was curious that even in his rational years the man who had conceived Funny Farms never seemed to produce another such original idea. This fact was probably as irksome to him as it was surprising to others. Certainly, it accounted for one of the two obsessions that eventually made it necessary for Cyrus to be 'institutionalized'; the last two years of his life were spent at a very private sanatorium in Florida – in local and appropriate parlance a 'funny farm'. The second fixation was so serious in the chairman of a public corporation that it qualified as an un-American activity: Cyrus began giving all the company's money away.

In his declining years Cyrus Hatch developed a concern for farming far exceeding in intensity any exhibited by the Department of Agriculture. Since he had abandoned the plough with no misgivings at the age of thirty-three, this turn of events must be accounted a delayed emotional throw-back, induced by lachrymose senility and overbearing nostalgia. Convinced that mechanization and chemicals were undermining rural husbandry and the moral fibre of the nation, Cyrus began funding a programme aimed at putting the clock back. He offered aid and countless unencumbered benefactions to farmers all over America in return for a simple pledge to observe the Funny Farms Pure Food Code. Broadly, the Code involved the eschewing of all mechanical implements and synthetic feeds, fertilizers and sprays down on the farm. If the whole farming community had adopted the principles involved, national food production would have dwindled to negligible quantities. Predictably, the vast majority of farmers and stockmen ignored the clarion call, the free plough horses, the three-legged milking stools, and the other nineteenth-century model-farm equipment on offer. A few however – mostly smallholders – were ready enough to accept the virtually unconditional cash grants

that went along with the equipment because this was infinitely more agreeable than working. As the numbers of
freeloaders grew, so did the apprehension of the Treasurer
at Funny Farms Inc. What had initially been regarded,
inside the company, as a harmless and possibly beneficial
public relations exercise, soon began to loom as an unendurable drain on corporate resources. When Wall
Street reached the same conclusion, action was instituted.

Cyrus Hatch was never declared insane. The indignity
and legal formalities thus avoided were traded for his
consenting to retire from the Company and take up permanent residence with Amelia at their winter home in
Florida. To the end of his days, spent at the nearby Sunny
Times Sanatorium, Cyrus remained legally responsible
for his own actions and arrangements despite the fact
that by this time he had assumed the identity of 'Farmer'
George – King of England from 1760 to 1820.

Thus it was that the legal propriety of the Funny Farms
Foundation was never in doubt. Indeed, the only person
who might have proved grounds for challenging its
validity – as well as its bizarre aims and objects – was
Amelia Hatch, the doting widow of its deranged founder.
Far from wishing to sully her late husband's image,
Amelia, who had never truly accepted that Cyrus had
been off his head, viewed the fulfilment of his wishes
through the Foundation as a fitting memorial to a very
fine human being.

It was in the months immediately following his en-
forced 'exile' to Florida that Cyrus Hatch had conceived
the notion of leaving his fortune to further a good cause.
He was, at the time, disenchanted with American
farmers in general, and with the Secretary of State for
Agriculture in particular; neither, through their recent
actions or attitudes, had afforded his Pure Food project
the acceptance and support it deserved.

A convinced Anglophile since his youthful wartime
sojourn in England, Cyrus determined that the British
nation should benefit substantially from his accumulated

wealth after his death. God might see fit to save America
and its revolting colonists, but Cyrus Hatch, like the
Third Hanoverian, was washing his soul of the whole
affair.

Having already provided for Amelia's well-being, Cyrus
elected to transfer the remainder of his fortune into the
Funny Farms Foundation. The object of the Foundation
was to fund, out of income, a Funny Farms Faculty of
Agriculture at some respectable institution for higher
education in Britain ready to accept both the money and
the peculiar conditions attaching. These last naturally
involved the recipient institution in forgoing involvement
or research in forms of agriculture and animal husbandry
that were not exclusively to do with the production of pure
food, unaffected and unadulterated by mechanical or
chemical intervention. Thus Cyrus hoped to underwrite a
return to Merrie England, complete with maidens dancing
around maypoles at the appropriate time, and to the
delight of menfolk clad in fustian smocks.

Needless to say, three years after the death of Cyrus
Hatch no 'respectable' British university had declared
itself ready to humour his wishes, the fulfilment of which,
on a big enough scale, would have put the nation on a
starvation diet or qualified it for receipt of international
famine relief. Existing agricultural faculties were for the
most part too involved in finding ways of fooling battery
hens into believing that dawn came twice a day to be
interested in pursuing lines of enquiry that could easily
involve those same creatures in discovering that legs could
be used for tearing around farmyards, burning up energy
earmarked for building up oven-ready bodies.

The advertised availability of approximately a million
dollars a year going spare for want of takers naturally
produced some interest from educationalists. Universities,
Polytechnics and other places of learning owning sound
provenance and status cooled to the proposition on learning the terms, but there was no shortage of applications
from the less worthy kind of establishments – some of

whom appeared to have been brought into being for the specific purpose of applying for the bounty. Predictably, none of the latter kind stood the test of preliminary examination by the educational agency in London appointed by the Funny Farms Foundation.

Indeed, the conscientious head of that respectable establishment, in personally visiting each applicant body, often found himself in strange places and curious company. One such visit was to a self-styled commercial college near Euston Station, where the exclusively female student body appeared to have been recruited entirely from Thailand and which, while not licensed by the Greater London Council, seemed to be licensed for almost everything else. Thus it was that this disillusioned gentleman, on returning from that very expedition, had his flagging spirits renewed by the unexpected but welcome application from University College, Itchendever. Not only was the College known to him, but also he had a very healthy respect for its achievements. On a different day, he might have debated whether an establishment devoted entirely to instruction in the liberal arts was truly poised for diversification into agriculture. Being fresh or, more appositely, stale from Euston, no such doubts assailed him. At least Itchendever was in the country, and indeed sat in fifty acres of the worst-kept parkland in England, described in the letter of application as admirably fallow in all senses. He looked up the train times to Winchester and wrote to Pittsburgh without delay.

CHAPTER II

AMELIA HATCH and Irvine J. Witaker stared in silent surprise at the open cardboard hat box. It lay where Witaker had uncovered it on a table in Amelia's suite at the Dorchester Hotel.

'The gift wrapping was pretty fancy,' Amelia was the first to speak, and in matter-of-fact tones, 'but it sure as hell didn't come from Harrods.'

'It's . . . it's disgusting.'

In Amelia's view, middle-aged attorneys-at-law with Ivy League pretensions and solid corporate practices tended to inhabit the sheltered side of life.

'No, Irv,' she said, employing a contraction Witaker suffered only from those he could not afford to correct. 'No, it's not disgusting; I'd say it was an eight-month Shropshire Down that ain't gonna see nine. Say, didn't you have lamb for dinner last night?'

The dead sheep's head stared balefully at the two from inside the box. Witaker looked away. The blood-soaked wrappings gave the severed head a gruesome appearance unlike anything he had seen either in a butcher's shop or mounted as a gun-room trophy. There was also the message.

'Keep away from UCI.' Amelia read this aloud from where it was hand-lettered in capitals on the inside of the box lid. 'Irv, I'd say whoever wrote this is trying to tell us something.'

Witaker found this piece of homespun levity distasteful and vulgar – a description that also happened to cover his opinion of Amelia Hatch. The three days he had already spent in his client's company had proved an eternity; the contemplation of at least three more was something he tried to avoid. There were times when he consoled himself with the thought that when the old baggage was finally

called to her reward – an event that surely to God could
not be long delayed – his own temporal benefit would be
substantial; this was such a time.

'The question is, what are we going to do about it?' he
asked, staring at the telephone, not because he had made
up his mind to use the instrument but rather because he
found its presence comforting, and its appearance somehow more agreeable than that of Mrs Hatch or the contents of the box.

'The sheep's head? Well, I guess we could have it
cooked. Mr Hatch always enjoyed a dish of sheep's
brains.'

It had long been Witaker's view that Mrs Hatch was
quite as unhinged as her late husband – a person to whom
she invariably referred in the formal style, even in conversation with one of her dear departed's few intimates.
Witaker found this habit irritating – and his irritation with
Mrs Hatch was developing into a fixation. Her inane
reply to his serious question was typical and infuriating.
He was nevertheless wrong about his client's state of mind,
and, indeed, in most of his emotionally inspired judge-
ments about her. Socially she embarrassed him; so had his
own mother, and for roughly the same reasons.

Amelia Hatch had been born and nurtured the daughter
of a poor hill farmer in the Allegheny Mountains. The
obligations inherent in a more affluent life-style she had
sanctioned grudgingly at first, seeing them as scarcely
justified against a code of Calvinistic frugality. The
propriety of wearing shoes in the summertime she had
conceded with ill grace at a fairly mature age. Possessions
like houses in the plural, automobiles by the herd, and
enough clothes to fill a mail order catalogue had been
tolerated before they were enjoyed – and because they
pleased Cyrus. Zeal was eventually tempered by a high-
toned regard for the responsibility devolving from wealth –
a common and convenient compromise – but Amelia
remained a country girl at heart, and above all a faithful
and loyal wife.

Hard-working almost to a fault, when the Funny Farms organization had consisted of two people operating in a single back room, it was Amelia who had laboured hardest – assembling, packing, despatching, keeping the accounts, giving no quarter to debtors, and holding the creditors at bay. Long after it was strictly necessary, she had continued to exercise or supervise many of these functions.

There were few people who appreciated how much Cyrus Hatch had owed his early success to the diligence of his wife, but Cyrus himself had harboured no doubts in the matter. Amelia had never embarrassed him with her country ways, even though she invariably projected the impression of having just stepped off the buck-board of a covered wagon, good and ready to boil the beans.

Witaker didn't care for beans, nor for this super-annuated, wizened frontierswoman with a penchant for chewing tobacco – in public. If, like Cyrus and Amelia, he had ever supped off sheep's head, it was something best forgotten. 'I think we should inform the police,' he said, still looking at the telephone.

'What, and have 'em laugh in our faces?' Amelia absently fingered one of the sheep's ears. 'Butchering a sheep's no federal offence in the States, and the English have been doing it for years.'

'Sending someone an obscene object with a threatening message is most certainly an offence in a civilized country.'

'Oh, come on, Irv; the whole thing's most probably a practical joke – some student at this college place, who's read about the trip, doesn't want our dough – and he's sure picked a colourful way of saying so.'

The news that the Funny Farms Foundation might be endowing University College, Itchendever, had appeared in several daily newspapers the day before. Its release had not been sanctioned by Witaker, and Grenwood, Phipps had stoutly denied making any announcement. The newspapers involved had refused to disclose the source but their information had been singularly accurate. They had even been told where to reach Mrs Hatch for confirmation – something she had gladly supplied, in detail, to all callers since she saw no reason for secrecy, and every cause for advertising the likely achievement of her late husband's chief ambition. She had not thought to consult Witaker in the matter, and in any case he had been sleeping off his jet-lag at the time Amelia had conducted what nearly amounted to a full-dress press conference. Witaker had been vexed by the event, and this irritation was renewed by the suggestion that it was spawning thoroughly undesirable repercussions.

The lawyer glanced briefly at the parcel. 'At least we can find out how the wretched thing got here. It didn't come by mail, so it must have been delivered by a messenger or a delivery service . . .'

'Quite the Sherlock Holmes, ain't you, Irv,' chided Amelia. 'Well, why don't you ask the hall porter when we go down – and, say, shouldn't we be on our way?' She climbed into an ancient, voluminous mink coat and crammed on a black straw hat. 'How do I look?' He thought she looked as though she had shot the pelts herself, and woven the hat from corn stubble. 'I've never had lunch at a *merchant* bank before, and I'm sure not going to be late,' Amelia continued. 'D'you suppose they wear aprons like grain merchants – and maybe trade money by weight?'

Witaker was not amused.

Mark Treasure was finding Mrs Hatch fascinating – quaint, but powerfully fascinating: like an early steam locomotive in working order. She had shown a lively and insatiable interest in the functions of the British merchant banking system, enquired intelligently about the law and process governing the flotation of companies, improved Treasure's own knowledge of the American Securities and Exchange Commission, and sensibly eschewed a visit to the computer with the dismissive comment, 'Ain't seen one yet that could tell a joke. Remember that, Mr

Treasure, computers can't laugh. That's what Mr Hatch used to say.'

In response to Treasure's very tentative offer of a drink before lunch, Amelia had, with alacrity, demanded rum and water in equal quantities. Having consumed this refreshment, she commended its medicinal and body-warming properties with such enthusiasm as to make her refusal of a second libation seem almost churlish. 'One's drinking; two's stinking – that's a good motto, Mr Treasure,' she had said with a laugh as she put down her empty glass.

Amelia was now waving a grouse leg at the banker and to the extreme discomfort of Witaker who was sitting on the other side of Treasure in the bank's dining-room. The chef had been advised tactfully to avoid foodstuffs commonly subjected to artificial improvement. It was coincidental that he had chosen dishes the consumption of which permitted the employment of fingers rather more than implements.

At the sight of the *moules marinières* Amelia had pinned her napkin to the cameo brooch at her throat and tucked in with enormous gusto. Grouse she declared to be a new experience, but clearly it was one she enjoyed. She had picked the tiny main carcase clean – to Witaker's great relief with her knife and fork – before applying herself to the manual dismemberment of what remained. 'Before I die, Mr Treasure; that's the point. Mr Hatch – rest his soul – wouldn't trust another living person to give away the fruits of his labour. Ain't that so, Irv?' Amelia directed an accusing glance at Witaker before returning her attention to the leg bone.

Witaker had been momentarily distracted – in both senses – by the reappearance of the butler carrying a bowl of walnuts. Amelia enjoyed cracking nuts with her bare hands; he thanked heaven there were none of a size she could tackle with her teeth, the soundness of which she had gratuitously advertised earlier. 'That is so, Mr Treasure,' he said, gathering his thoughts. 'Mrs Hatch and

I are the sole trustees of the Funny Farms Foundation, but, as you may know, unless the university faculty is arranged before her . . . er . . . her demise, the Foundation will be liquidated and the funds dispersed.'

Treasure had been made aware of all these facts – indeed they had been included in the newspaper reports – but the significance of the last detail was only now becoming clear to him.

'What Irv means is, if I kick the bucket before we get this show on the road, the money gets divided up between a bunch of great-nieces and nephews – worst thing that could happen to 'em. Andrew Carnegie said that; he was right too. Inherited wealth's the most corrupting thing on earth. Don't misunderstand me, Mr Treasure; I ain't no Commie, no sir, but wealth's a privilege that needs to be earned to be appreciated.'

Treasure did not find himself entirely out of sympathy with this sincerely pronounced philosophy. However, he was concentrating upon it less than upon the thought that the business in hand was dependent on the survival of a lady he judged to be in her mid-seventies.

Amelia guessed at this speculation. 'You're thinking this old bird – and I don't mean the grouse – is about ready for the scrap heap, Mr Treasure, so you'd better get a move on. You're right too. But you maybe won't find Irv so anxious; can't blame him though – y'see, his daughter's married to one of Mr Hatch's great-nephews.'

Treasure doubted that Witaker could let this last intelligence pass without comment. He was right; the lawyer cut in quickly. 'It was a measure of the late Mr Hatch's faith in my objectivity that he asked me . . . indeed, he insisted on my accepting the trusteeship with Mrs Hatch *after* my daughter's marriage.' Witaker had said his piece dispassionately, but Treasure detected a hint of unsureness in the tone.

'Then Mr Hatch evidently had very great faith in your judgement,' said the banker, and he meant it.

'Oh shoot, of course he did,' put in Amelia. 'I was only

kidding Irv. Fact remains, Mr Treasure, in three years we
haven't had an application for the endowment that's worth
a second look, let alone the trouble of me and Irv making
the trip over – 'cepting this one we're here about now.'

'The terms are a little unusual,' commented Treasure
drily, and without indicating he considered them just short
of ridiculous. 'You are quite right, though, to be selective
about the applications. So far as I know, University
College, Itchendever, is an entirely worthy institution –
how worthy you will have to judge for yourselves. To be
honest, I find it a trifle embarrassing that we are the
London correspondents of your bankers in Pittsburgh, in
view of Lord Grenwood's close connection with the
College; no doubt he would express the same view if he
were here.'

In fact, all Treasure's doubts lay in the opposite direction and he was glad to offer his last opinion without then
having spoken to George Grenwood whose later enthusiastic reception of the proposition was entirely lacking in
the lofty considerations of propriety credited to him by his
circumspect colleague.

'You come highly recommended, Mr Treasure,' said
Amelia, biting into a Cox's Orange Pippin and chomping
at it with a grace Witaker deemed worthy of a cart-horse.
'I think Lord Grenwood's connection with the place is one
of the best things we've heard about it.' She began
sizing up the walnuts.

Out of pure, personal curiosity, Treasure determined to
bring the conversation back to a part of the business on
which he considered he had been inadequately briefed.
He addressed his question to Witaker. 'In the event you
don't find a suitable establishment for the endowment,
you say the Foundation funds can eventually be dispersed.
Isn't that difficult in law?'

'Not in this particular case, Mr Treasure. I drew up
the trust deed myself; in the circumstances you predicate,
the trust fund becomes discretionary with the bank replacing Mrs Hatch as a second trustee. There would be a

certain amount due in extra taxes, mostly covered by the income that's accumulating.'

'What Irv means,' cut in Mrs Hatch, 'is that Mr Hatch's great-nieces and nephews would come in for a tidy sum each.'

'How many of them are there?' asked Treasure.

'Nine that we know of,' answered Amelia, and Treasure attached no particular significance to the qualification in her reply.

Lunch concluded, Treasure had politely seen Mrs Hatch and Witaker to their hired Daimler before making towards his office. It had been agreed he would drive down to Itchendever independently to meet them there at noon on the following day. Amelia had expressed a desire to start early in order to 'take in' Winchester Cathedral on the way, as well as the village of Bishop's Oak, near Eastleigh Airport, where Cyrus had been billeted for several months during 1917. Witaker did not share this desire, but he was not consulted.

Miss Gaunt, Treasure's invaluable secretary, was a maiden lady of sober habits with a disposition equal to coping with special crises as coolly as with normal business. Although she lacked the youth and beauty that could lure men into – or conceivably out of – burning buildings, her employer would have rescued her from any peril in gratitude for service rendered and in protection of more to come. It was thus the more surprising for Treasure to find Miss Gaunt taut, trembling, and tight-lipped in his outer office, facing an evidently bewildered Sergeant Smith, the Grenwood, Phipps' uniformed senior doorman.

The Sergeant was holding the lid of a long cardboard box of the type used by florists. The box itself lay open on Miss Gaunt's desk.

As he entered the room Treasure heard his secretary say, in uncharacteristic, emotional tones, 'Well, if it was addressed to Lord Grenwood, *his* secretary should be

dealing with it.' She turned to Treasure, dabbing the side
of her mouth with a linen handkerchief. 'Please excuse me
for a moment, Mr Treasure,' she said, and hurried into the
corridor clearly in a state of high distress.

'What's up, Sergeant Smith?' asked Treasure, closing
the door behind the fleeing figure of his secretary.

The Sergeant saluted smartly. 'This 'ere box, sir, was
delivered by a lad just after the dinner hour. I took it up
to his Lordship's secretary personal, sir. She 'ad a look at it
and sent me on to you, sir.'

Lord Grenwood's successive secretaries were invariably
glamorous, and usually incompetent. How long they
stayed depended on how soon after their appointment
Lady Grenwood visited her husband at the office, which
in turn depended on how successful he was at persuading
her he was somewhere else. Treasure, to his credit, could
not recall whether the present incumbent was blonde or
brunette – in either case it was safe to assume the girl
would not know how to deal with a problem that had later
defeated the resourceful Miss Gaunt. He took the box lid
from the Sergeant. Written on it, in spidery capitals, was
the message 'Keep FFF off UCI'.

Treasure moved to the desk, and gazed down upon the
contents of the box – a rope of gristly, pinkish flesh on a
gory bed of tissue paper. 'What the devil is it, Sergeant?'
he asked.

'Well, sir, as I was trying to explain to Miss Gaunt,'
replied Sergeant Smith, whose father had been a porter at
Smithfield Market, 'unless I'm mistaken, sir, that's the . . .
er . . . the . . . er . . .' The Sergeant swallowed. 'The
private part of a bull, sir.'

CHAPTER III

ITCHENDEVER HALL – the home of University College – is
Greek Revival running to seed. It was designed by William
Wilkins in 1830 for a rich Southampton merchant much
taken by the grandeur of The Grange, a house by the
same architect a few miles to the north. Sadly, while The
Grange – one of Wilkins's early works – is much admired,
commentators tend to dismiss the Hall as a trivial,
decadent, dummy run for the National Gallery – a building they consider immensely more trivial (because it is
bigger), created by Wilkins two years later.

The fact remains that laymen find the Hall a pretty
place, and infinitely more pleasing than the imitation
Gothic piles that ten years after its erection were *de
rigueur* as homes for parvenus in search of instant provenance. Built on elevated ground overlooking a natural lake,
the Hall, on its southern façade, comprises eleven pavilions and bays, dominated by a central, octastyle Corinthian portico, pedimented and topped by a squat dome.
Each of the two terminal pavilions has its own smaller
dome, a feature more practical and admittedly less
obviously absurd than the ornamental turrets used by
Wilkins to top off the ends of the National Gallery.

Whatever its weaknesses, Itchendever Hall has survived
– the scholarship and taste there still intact – and for a
better reason than the mere provision of a subject for
carping, purist analysis. In the late 1950s, when
higher education was all the rage, the building was pur-
chased and endowed – partly out of local and central
government funds, partly by public subscription – to form
the nucleus of a new university. But the project foundered
a few years later. New, though nasty, purpose-built
establishments were by then considered more wholesome
settings for young seekers after truth and learning than

places that might conceivably corrupt the atmosphere
with the smell of history and blocked drains. Money
intended to enable University College, Itchendever, to
extend its curricula from the liberal arts into the sciences
was diverted into other academic channels. Laboratories
remained unbuilt, libraries were not extended, extra
student accommodation became a pipe dream, and the
lavatories remained inadequate – even though, taken
individually, they are among the most commodious in
Britain.

No one actually demanded the closure of the College.
Up to 1974, at least, there were still too many students
chasing too few university places for the Department of
Education formally to approve a reduction in the number
of higher educational establishments. There was also the
embarrassing circumstance that year after year all
hundred-odd finalists at the College obtained firsts – or
else good second-class degrees. This evidence of academic
excellence was given little advertisement by those in
authority. It stood in such sharp contrast to results
obtained elsewhere as to make comparison invidious and
enquiry acutely perplexing to enlightened educationalists.

University College had fewer than three hundred
students. Its facilities were limited. Local and central
authority had long since ceased giving it money. Many of
its students had to rely on their parents and vacation
work for subsistence because most county councils refused
them the grants available to those studying at 'fully
recognized' establishments. There was no record of rioting
at the College which was too small to attract the organiz-
ing talents of the National Union of Students. Loafers and
lame-brains were 'sent down' for not working, without
protest from anyone – a process that served to concentrate the minds of those wishing to stay, and one that
underwrote the unsullied record of scholastic achievement. The resident staff of fifteen tutors, supplemented by
ten visiting academics from other establishments as far
afield as Reading and Brighton, were over-worked, under-

paid, but dedicated.

Itchendever, being in the heart of the country, offered few distractions, but the small, close-knit, industrious community owned one highly attractive compensation. The student body was equally divided between men and women. Outdoor sports held few attractions for those in residence.

Mark Treasure was scarcely aware of the unique qualities attaching to University College as the chauffeur-driven Rolls-Royce swung into the main drive of Itchendever Hall. But he was delighted by the sight and quality of the English Renaissance building that commanded the view across the lake the car was skirting. The early November sunlight, the white stone, the rolling green parkland, the leafless trees – saving for a few bronzed oaks stoutly defending the retreat of autumn – the shimmering water, all combined to form the placid landscape he had been actively anticipating during the hour-long journey. It was then that the lady fell off her bicycle, causing Henry Pink to swerve and stop with an alacrity customarily associated with Trafalgar Square in the rush hour.

Pink glanced round at his employer. 'I never touched her, sir.'

Treasure was already out of the car, making for the tangled mound of tweed, machinery, and stout flailing legs fetched up on the verge a yard ahead of where the car had stopped. His approach was momentarily arrested by the emergence from the pile of an enormous black cat – back arched, fur raised, teeth bared – that sprang into a sentinel position before the confused mass. Treasure had never seen such a large cat. It hissed at him venomously.

'Tottle, behave.' This command had no evident effect upon the cat, and came in a rich contralto from underneath the bicycle.

Risking the feline threat, Treasure advanced upon the disentangling heap in time to assist the robust, dishevelled, and aged owner of the voice to her feet.

'He'll do you no harm . . . thank you so much . . . his
real name's Aristotle, Tottle for short . . . naughty
Tottle . . . I *am* so sorry.' All this the lady delivered
breathlessly. 'Oh, so kind of you . . . all our fault, I'm
afraid.' This last was directed at Pink who was doing his
best to straighten the handlebars of a pre-war Hercules
lady's cycle with a lyrically swooping crossbar, and a huge
wicker basket that hung drunkenly, one securing strap
broken, over the front wheel. 'There's the cause of our
misadventure,' continued its human victim, tapping the
severed strap with a firm forefinger. 'And perhaps poor
Tottle was only trying to trim the ship.'

'Are you in one piece?' Treasure was already reason-
ably sure that the stout, matriarchal figure, thickly clad
in matching cloak, coat and skirt of heavyweight Scottish
woollens, had emerged unscathed from the spill.

'Right enough, thank you so much. Just a bit winded,
don't you know. I must introduce myself . . . Miss Stopps,
Margaret Stopps. Now, let me see, you'll be Mr Treasure.'
Miss Stopps dropped her right shoulder and lunged
forward as though about to add ample wing-forward
support in the third row. Treasure found his hand
enveloped in a tight grip almost before he was aware of
having raised it.

'How do you do.' Treasure paused. 'I'm afraid you
have the advantage . . .'

'Quite so, Mr Treasure,' interrupted Miss Stopps, with
a confident smirk, as though this were a common enough
experience. She used both hands to lift a wide-brimmed
felt hat off her head, revealing a shock of short, wavy,
grey hair, before cramming the hat back on with some
force. 'Intelligent deduction on my part; invited to lunch
with the Dean to meet the benefactors – and clearly
you're not Mrs . . . er . . . Mrs Hatch. False economy not
to come in the car, of course, but Tottle prefers the bike.'

Since it was doubtful that Tottle had been asked to
lunch, Treasure assumed the formidable animal might
customarily be used to guard whatever conveyance its

owner chose to employ. 'I'm hardly a benefactor, I'm
afraid,' he said. 'Just an adviser to Mrs Hatch. Are you in
some way associated with the College, Miss Stopps?'

'Merely what you might call a well-wisher,' replied the
lady. She opened her arms wide towards the lake and the
Hall in a Valkyrian gesture made the more dramatic by
the cloak. 'Isn't it a simply magnificent sight, Mr
Treasure? So well worth preserving; oh, so very well
worth preserving.' Miss Stopps delivered the last part of
this statement almost to herself. She pursed her lips
together firmly, lower jaw thrust out, strong square chin
set determinedly. She rounded on the banker. 'You'll do
what you can, Mr Treasure? We must all do what we
can.'

'Of course,' replied Treasure, not quite certain what it
was Miss Stopps was expecting of him. 'This is my first
visit; the house is even more beautiful than I had imagined.'

'Quite so; they say the architect liked it best by moonlight – the reflection in the lake and so forth. Shall you
stay for the fireworks? Six o'clock; I do hope so.'

Treasure had no intention of dining as well as lunching
at the College, had quite overlooked that it was November
the fifth, and loathed fireworks. 'It's improbable I'll be
here so late, I'm afraid,' he replied.

'Well, perhaps we can persuade Mrs Hatch to watch
our little display. I suppose Americans would know about
Guy Fawkes? – or perhaps not.' Miss Stopps pointed
across the lake without waiting for Treasure's own conjecture. 'The undergraduates arrange some quite beautiful tableaux of pyrotechnics; they're starting to put up the
scaffolding now in front of the Hall – so ingenious. Just
one example of the splendid collegiate spirit here, Mr
Treasure.'

They stepped into the road the better to view the group
activity in which Miss Stopps took such pride – and were
very nearly run over. A black Cadillac of enormous
dimensions appeared almost silently from behind the

Rolls and glided past, at no great speed, but nevertheless perilously close to the pair, whose attentions had not been concentrated on traffic flow. The uniformed driver slowed the big car to a crawl so that Treasure, removing himself and his companion to safety, still had time to observe the three other occupants, none of whom appeared to be the least bit interested in him or his well-being.

Sitting alone on the back seat of the Cadillac was an obviously noble Arab in full national regalia. The centre row of seats – for it was that kind of car – was occupied by two swarthy heavyweights in western clothes. Treasure correctly assumed these two to be bodyguards, and immediately set himself guessing as to the identity of the august personage requiring full-scale protection in the heart of rural Hampshire. The banker did a great deal of business in the Middle East, and he made it part of this business to meet most of the really important visitors to London from the many Arab states where Grenwood, Phipps was heavily involved. He was fairly certain that the chief occupant of the car was not from one of these. It intrigued him that the man should drive into the country dressed and attended in a style appropriate to an official occasion, or at least one where status required underlining. Most of his wealthy Arab acquaintances cultivated anonymity when in England; a lasting source of satisfaction, as well as income, to those who laboured in Savile Row. The car bore no diplomatic emblems, and the number plate was American.

Treasure turned to Miss Stopps. 'Are the fireworks to be followed by a performance of *The Desert Song*?'

'What a droll and original observation, Mr Treasure.' Miss Stopps's large frame shook with mirth. 'Alas, nothing of the sort is planned, at least, not until the end of term when we have our revue,' she added earnestly, no doubt as further evidence of extra-mural *esprit*. 'This year it will be called *Itchen All Over* – a play on words, d'you see?' And without waiting for Treasure fully to savour this waggery, she continued. 'Unless I am mistaken, that was the Crown Prince of Abu B'yat.'

'Indeed,' said Treasure, impressed with the information but more so by the knowledge of its purveyor. 'And is he a frequent visitor?'

'I think not. He has a son here – a nice lad, not bright, but agreeably unpretentious.' Treasure wondered whether perhaps Miss Stopps did some tutoring as part of her well-wisher role. 'The boy was intended for Oxford but there was some misunderstanding – I believe leading to altercation – about his entrance qualifications. It was something of a coup when the Dean attracted him here.'

Treasure agreed, though Miss Stopps's last point implied that University College, Itchendever, was not above lowering its academic guard in the cause of celebrity.

Abu B'yat was one of the smallest of the Persian Gulf Emirates, but certainly one of the richest. It was exceptional in that its ruler demonstrated little faith in the British economy. Only a tiny proportion of Abu B'yat's huge oil revenues were invested in London, quite the largest portion being placed in the USA. In common with the rest of the British banking community, Treasure had long since ceased to work, or hope, for a change in attitude on the part of the ruling Emir. Now he speculated on the likelihood of the situation altering with the succession of a Crown Prince whose regard for English education at least seemed proof against American competition. Treasure testily wondered also why he had been reduced to gleaning this interesting intelligence through a chance meeting with a maiden lady in Hampshire when his company supported a whole department charged to keep him posted on just such highly portentous information.

Miss Stopps drew Treasure aside with the air of a conspirator, although except for Pink, the chauffeur, who was busy at the rear of the Rolls-Royce, they were a quarter of a mile from any other visible human contact. 'A word in confidence, Mr Treasure,' she said in a subdued voice, after glancing both ways along the drive. 'It is rumoured – and I must emphasize it is only rumour – that the Crown Prince may be planning to buy the College.' This titbit offered, Miss Stopps drew back, eyes narrowed, the better it seemed to watch the morsel being digested.

'To *buy* the College! But surely that would be impossible?' questioned the putative stand-in for the institution's Chairman of Trustees.

'Not at all, Mr Treasure.' Miss Stopps was again adopting her conspiratorial attitude. 'The authorities,' she continued, without specifying which bodies the phrase encompassed, 'are ignorant enough to regard the College as a financial embarrassment, and sufficiently profligate to dispose of it, if a face-saving opportunity arose.' She paused. 'So it seems we may be flattered by the presence of two potential benefactors today.'

'And not by coincidence.' Treasure was beginning to catch up with the events that had so far overtaken him.

'Indeed not. Your own visit with Mrs Hatch has been much advertised of late. If there is substance in the rumour about the Crown Prince's intentions, then your visit has no doubt precipitated his.'

This, thought Treasure, would also account for the Prince's finery and the size of his entourage – natural scene-setting for an important Arab with a purchase in mind.

'Well, Mr Treasure, I must delay you no longer with my spills and confidences. It has been a great pleasure, and, of course, we shall meet again at lunch. Before then I have a meeting with the Entertainments Committee.' Miss Stopps closely examined the dial of a gold, half-hunter watch which she had produced from a capacious knitting bag suspended around her neck by a woollen cord. 'Goodness, I'm late . . . Oh, thank you so much; how clever of you.'

Pink, at whom the expression of gratitude was aimed, had secured the basket to the handlebars of the bicycle with a piece of stout twine produced from the boot of the car. Miss Stopps scooped up Tottle, and deposited him in the basket with a marked absence of ceremony. She then mounted the bicycle, and after a wobbly start, set off down the drive, upright in the saddle, with Tottle intently examining the front wheel from his point of vantage.

CHAPTER IV

FIONA TRIGG, tall and twenty, angularly beautiful, and nicely developed in all the right places, stood buttoning up her blouse near the first-floor sitting-room window. 'I *am* properly dressed – and anyway, no one can see me. Darling, you are getting prissy in your old age.' She glanced over her shoulder at Peter Gregory – who was all of twenty-seven – smirked, pushed her owlish spectacles further up the bridge of her nose, and returned her attention to the scene in the courtyard below. 'It's the biggest car I've ever seen . . . and it *is* Faisal's father, I told you so.'

The lanky, bearded Australian she was addressing promptly put down the beer glasses he was carrying, hurried to the door, and turned the key in the lock.

'Oh, Mr Gregory, now I'm in your power,' cried the girl in mock dismay. 'Unlock the door immediately or I shall tell my tutor.'

'I *am* your tutor,' came the over-melodramatic reply from the University College Reader in English Literature. He crossed the room, grasped Fiona from behind, and drew her away from the window. 'And I'm only protecting you from marauding Arabs.'

'My hero!' She twisted around in his arms, took off her glasses, and kissed him briefly on the lips. 'And you should have locked the door half an hour ago.' He wasn't paying attention. 'Now who's looking out of the window? . . . Peter, they're not likely to try busting in here, are they?'

'Those two muscle-men look capable of anything, and they've got a hamper big enough to put you in.' Peter was watching the occupants of the Cadillac as they disembarked, and made for the staircase he shared with Sheikh Al Haban's son in the quadrangle of what had been the stable block of Itchendever Hall. The building stood some fifty yards to the north of the Hall, and had been converted to provide living accommodation for students. There were some larger sets of rooms for junior teaching staff. The Crown Prince's son had been afforded one of these in view of his status and – literally – because he could afford it.

The elegantly planned courtyard, three-storeyed on all sides, grassed in the centre, with pedimented arch exit on the Hall side, recalled the atmosphere and arrangement of an Oxford College quadrangle. Access for motor vehicles was possible but forbidden. No one had yet appeared ready to make this point to the owner of the Cadillac that compactly provided more horse-power than the nineteenth-century stables had ever housed.

'Was Faisal expecting his father?' Fiona had moved to the sofa where she was now curled, blue-jeaned and barefoot, sipping lager from a glass tankard.

'Not that I know of . . . leastways he didn't mention it this morning. He was here just before you came. Hell, I hope he's in, otherwise the Arab Legion *will* be banging on my door. Listen a minute.'

The sound of heavy footsteps on the uncarpeted, wooden staircase ended. There were voices raised in greeting on the landing; the noise of doors opening and shutting. Fiona nodded reassuringly at her tutor. 'D'you think he's here to outwit the dreaded Funny Farms woman – sorry, your venerable great-aunt – in the nick of time, buy the joint, and move in with the camels?'

'Not funny,' replied the Australian, 'and I've told you to forget the great-aunt bit; that information was strictly confidential. So far as I'm concerned there's no relationship, or none that's going to be acknowledged. After the way the Hatch family treated my mother I can do without any connection with any of 'em, thank you very much.'

'And just because she became a Catholic . . .'

'Bigots, the lot of them; my grandfather especially, by all accounts. Anyway, it's all ancient history so far as I'm concerned . . . If my mother hadn't run away to San

Francisco in the war, she'd never have met my father, she wouldn't have become an Australian, and I wouldn't be here now . . .'

'With me.'

'With you.' He smiled at the girl.

'And her family still don't even know your mother's in Australia?'

'They don't even know she's alive – and I don't suppose they care either.'

'Well, I think that's simply awful,' said Fiona with great feeling. She brightened. 'Was your father in the regular Australian Navy then? I mean, I know he's in sheep now.'

'No, he was a reserve officer – hostilities only. And he's not "in sheep" like your father's "in the City". He's just an ordinary small sheep farmer.'

'Will they like me – your mother and father, d'you think? I mean, when we're married . . .'

'Who says we're getting married?' Peter tried to register surprise.

'I do,' said the girl firmly, with a satisfied grin. 'That was settled ages ago, otherwise I wouldn't have let you . . . Well, anyway, answer the question; will they like me?'

'More than your father's going to like me – a penniless lecturer from the Antipodes.' He made the last syllable rhyme with 'roads'.

'Absolute tosh; Daddy's a darling, and he'll love you. He's not a bit snobbish . . .'

'There you are . . .'

'Oh, stop being obtuse.' Fiona glanced at her watch. 'Hey, it's nearly twelve. You should charge extra for two-hour tutorials.' He moved towards the sofa. 'No, too late; it's time to finish dressing for the top persons' lunch.' Peter shrugged his shoulders in reply; the girl giggled. 'Well, at least put a shirt on.'

A mile away in what Mrs Hunter-Smith insisted on calling the drawing-room of Number One, The Cottages, in Itchendever village, Major Reginald Hunter-Smith,

Bursar of University College, was doing his best to leave for the same event that summoned Peter Gregory. He, at least, was already suitably dressed for the occasion, complete with regimental tie: it was not a well-known regiment, and one that had long since forgotten his existence, but the tie, like the military title, was essential to the wearer's carefully contrived persona.

'You've fluffed it again, you bloody idiot.'

'Winifred, I must go . . . I'll be late . . .'

'Then be late, go sick, do anything if it'll help put this old woman off Itchendever. Reginald – ' the huge bosom heaved under the lambswool twin set – 'you are no longer part of University College. You are Business Director elect of Torchester Polytechnic – there's the letter on your desk; read it again . . .'

'My love, I don't need to read it again . . .'

'Then get it into your head that you owe these people nothing. Four years you've worked here, and what have we got to show for it?'

'It's better than that public relations job . . .'

'Don't be irrelevant. If it hadn't been for you, UCI would never have heard of the Funny Farms Foundation, let alone applied for the money. If Torchester are going to apply, then it's in your interests to see they get it – and that UCI doesn't. It'll give you a flying start there – on top of the seven thousand a year.'

'But I don't even take up the appointment until September – and I haven't given the Dean my notice yet.'

'All the more reason for underselling UCI to Mrs Snatch . . .'

'Mrs Hatch.'

'All right, Mrs Hatch; all the more reason why they won't think it fishy if you steer her off Itchendever today. Are you certain that Torchester have put in their application?'

'Oh, quite. The head of their Agriculture Department was absolutely sold on my idea for using the money. He said it was brilliant – solved all the problems they saw when they first thought of applying two years ago . . .'

'There you are – brilliant. You say he said you were brilliant . . .'

'Well, he didn't mean . . .'

'Never mind what he meant. Just don't go and give the same ideas to Itchendever, and most of all, don't do a thing that'll encourage Mrs Snatch to put the money here. You've got to sell her *off*, Reginald – get it into your head – off, off. Now get going or you'll be late.'

'Yes, my love.'

'A miracle we've survived at all, Mr Treasure . . . more sherry? . . . please do . . . oh, I'm sorry . . . here, take my handkerchief. Yes, continued acceptance by the CNAA – the Council for National Academic Awards, you know – is absolutely essential to us . . . our numbers are so small, you understand, they might well consider us under strength for degree recognition at any time. My own influence in that quarter has been vital . . .'

Eric Ribble, MA, Dean of University College and Head of the English Department, bobbed up and down nervously in front of Treasure, brandishing a decanter like a conductor's baton. Short, chubby, and evidently well-meaning, Treasure had branded him Pickwickian on first acquaintance. This good-natured assessment was now under review. Treasure disliked verbosity almost as much as sherry; he was suffering a surfeit of both.

Since the unceasing torrent of words to which the banker had been subjected for all of ten minutes allowed neither for interlocution nor even interruption, he decided stoically to let it flow over him, like the last ministration of sherry, and – apart from an occasional nod of approval matched to the cadence of the speaker's voice – engage his attention in observing those others present in the crowded Senior Common Room.

Mrs Hatch was close by, dressed in the identical garments she had been wearing the day before, including the moth-eaten mink coat which she had refused to discard on arrival, exclaiming 'Holy mackerel, when's the heating coming on?' Thus she had not only secured standing room before the large open log fire but also – after loud demand – a glass of rum and water, the production of which made Treasure wish he had swallowed hesitation instead of sherry and asked for a whisky and soda in the first place.

Amelia was talking to a tall, dark, mountain of a man with a severe and fleshy countenance, clad in a jacket and trousers that might arguably have pre-dated the mink. Treasure had needed no formal introduction immediately to have recognized Daniel Goldstein when he entered the room. Senior Tutor and Head of the History Department, Dr Goldstein was an academic of some note and the author of several learned works on obscure aspects of antiquity. All this paled, however, beside the fact that he appeared regularly on television in what had originally been intended as a middle-brow programme entitled *Verdict on History*. This fortnightly event allowed historians and politicians in contention to examine important characters from the past – often the very recent past – and to reassess their contribution to civilization in the light of the most up-to-date evidence. The programme had come to enjoy a tremendous following, much to the delight and surprise of the television contractors responsible for its invention, who smugly accepted plaudits for cultural involvement while joyfully banking an unexpected bonus in advertising revenue.

In truth the success of the programme had less to do with the public's thirst for historical enlightenment than with its delight in the performances of the abrasive Dr Goldstein – the regular 'anchor man'. To him no institution or person – living or dead – was sacred. He had proved to be the arch debunker of popularist politicians, generals and statesmen with his uncanny knack for exposing the Achilles' heels that left clay feet unprotected.

The viewing public delighted in these twice-monthly character assassinations and the caustic, witty, irreverent,

hot-tempered, and brilliant Dr Goldstein became – in
television parlance – 'a hot property'. Nor was there any
risk that he might become over-exposed. Immune to
better offers, from the academic as well as the entertain-
ment world, Goldstein elected to continue teaching in a
relatively unknown educational establishment, to per-
severe in the compiling of yet further treatises on obscure
subjects, to spend some part of his summer vacation
labouring like a peasant on an Israeli kibbutz, and to
refuse requests to appear in quiz programmes or to write
pre-digested historical philosophy for paperback pub-
lishers. In short, Dr Goldstein knew his limitations,
recognized the singularity of the formulae that underwrote the success of *Verdict on History*, did not care for the
atmosphere of large universities – which seemed always to
inflame his natural acerbity – and was entirely satisfied
with his life at Itchendever.

Mrs Hatch knew nothing of these matters, nor had she
ever heard of Dr Goldstein, who was now listening to her
with stony tolerance and mounting horror.

Witaker was with his client, looking less apprehensive
than was customary when obliged to accompany Mrs
Hatch into polite society. He, too, was allowing his mind
to wander – even to reminisce. The evening before he had
spent on a personal inspection of some other educational
establishments that had applied for the Funny Farms
Foundation endowment, but which had been found want-
ing. Of the three listed that time and distance allowed
him to include, two he viewed only from the outside. The
third – the commercial college near Euston Station, and
the one that interested him most from the reports – he had
entered and examined closely for all of two hours, naturally without revealing his identity. In the event he was
quite satisfied with the accuracy of the earlier report.
Indeed, he had been so entirely satisfied that he aimed to
return as quickly as possible for yet more satisfaction of a
type that his sensual, sadistic propensities made irresistible.
Witaker was truly a man of hidden depths – as well

hidden as the man who had followed and logged his movements throughout the previous evening.

Across the room Miss Stopps, who had just arrived, was chatting earnestly with Major Reginald Hunter-Smith, together with a bearded young man who had entered with her. Treasure knew that Hunter-Smith had been the instigator of the College's application to the Funny Farms Foundation. In a short conversation he had found the ex-officer businesslike but limited. He evidently enjoyed a celebrity as the College's man of affairs, a status probably not hard to achieve in a community of academics.

The Crown Prince of Abu B'yat had not put in an appearance, which prompted Treasure to assume he had not been invited to lunch or else – perish the thought – that the promised repast was not yet imminent.

'. . . multiplied by three hundred students produces an income of only £250,000 a year.' Ribble was babbling onwards. 'That sum is quite insufficient for our needs. We cannot increase the fees since a number of the students do receive discretionary grants from their local education authorities – not as a right, you understand, oh dear me no.' As though to emphasize the inequity in his last report, Ribble was seized by a sneezing fit.

Treasure grasped his opportunity. 'Tell me, do you have a rich Arab aiming to take you over?'

Ribble looked up from his handkerchief. 'That possibility does exist, but I assure you it is remote. Might I ask who told you . . .?'

'Oh, it's of no consequence,' Treasure cut in loyally. 'I thought I saw the Crown Prince of Abu B'yat earlier. Is he joining us for lunch?'

'Certainly not,' replied Ribble with such force as to imply that he might have some conscientious objection to breaking bread with upstart camel drivers. 'Sheikh Al Haban does happen to be here today, visiting his son. The boy has a special set of rooms in the stable quad – very commodious and proper. Food is prepared there for

parental visits . . . the religious considerations and so on.
The coincidence of this visit with your own is . . . er . . . is
inopportune. I fear I shall have to give the Sheikh a token
of my time this afternoon . . . a progress report on his
son . . .'

Treasure was delighted at this last intelligence, which
indicated that the meeting planned for later would not
consist of an uninterrupted soliloquy by the Dean. 'Quite
a feather in your cap, Dean, to have bagged a prince for
the College,' he put in loudly on the chance of altering the
direction if not the flow of the verbal tide.

Ribble appeared surprisingly perplexed by the compliment. 'I thought so at the time, yes . . .'

'And now his tiger's got us by the shorts.' Daniel
Goldstein had come to join them, and had overheard the
last exchange. 'If this nonsensical farm business gets
squashed today – and I sincerely hope to ensure it does –
then our next alternative to soldiering on unaided is to let
Al Haban gobble us up and turn us into a sort of finishing
school for the dimmer offspring of Middle Eastern poten-
tates. Won't work, of course, as Ribble here is perfectly
well aware. We'd lose our recognition in five minutes –
not to mention our credibility.'

The Dean looked both disconcerted and annoyed.
'Daniel, that was a singularly indelicate statement, even
for you. It was also misleading and inaccurate.'

CHAPTER V

THE LUNCHTIME meeting of the Junior Common Room Committee had been called at short notice and was proceeding with little formality in a corner of the bar at The Trout in Itchendever. The seven elected members present constituted a quorum, but no one had bothered to count; the Secretary was amongst those absent – he and two others were in any case excused since they were gainfully employed putting up the scaffolding for the fire-work display.

'It's agreed then that we're rejecting the CIA money *and* the Arab take-over.' Philip Clark, the JCR President, was Scottish, resolute, and anxious to get away to the cosy afternoon he had planned with his girl-friend.

There was a murmur of assent from the others, led understandably by Sarah Green who was the girl-friend in question.

'We don't *know* it's CIA money,' said a short, dark girl who was currently unattached, and who had nothing more pressing than a history essay to complete.

'Of course it's CIA money,' put in a confident male. 'There's no other organization in the world could have cooked up anything as zany and transparent . . .'

'And so unworkable it has to be a front for something else.' There were general nods of approval at this un-supported conjecture from a student of economics.

'Faisal's all right.' This, from the short, dark girl, was judged by the others to be more an indication of amatory aspirations than a considered opinion on the propriety of having University College ruled from Abu B'yat. The remark was consequently ignored.

'It's also agreed that Roger's in charge of the protest tonight.'

'Yes,' said Sarah Green promptly, eager to provide

support for the President – preferably without further delay.

Roger Dribdon was the JCR Secretary, and since he was already engaged in constructing a key contribution to the paraphernalia of protest, it may be assumed that the outcome of the meeting was a foregone conclusion. It would nevertheless be wrong to judge that any decision had been taken lightly. The resolution here properly approved – and later minuted by the absent Roger – had been the subject of wide discussion amongst a much larger section of the student body than those in attendance at The Trout. On the previous evening, and well into the night, soundings had been taken, groups convened, points argued. The JCR Committee was a democratically-elected body which traditionally avoided behaving in an oligarchic style on issues where conscience, principle, or the possibility of official retribution demanded reference back to the voters. An agreement to protest qualified under all three headings – and most particularly the last.

For reasons already stated, the student body at University College, Itchendever, was not normally given to protest, nor, in the memory of any of its members, had the JCR Committee ever before felt such a pressing obligation to take what almost amounted to a referendum on a special issue. With one or two exceptions, the members of the committee were by temperament and inclination entirely unsuited to provide radical leadership on subjects sterner than the pricing of drinks in the JCR bar or the size of subsidy deserved by the Film Society. It was not so much that the committee was passive as that it was rarely required to be active. People were elected to it who could be relied upon to provide a social service – not to stir up trouble. It was significant that even the course of action ratified over beer and sandwiches at The Trout had been adopted not simply on the strength of student opinion but also in secret collusion with some who might be said to exercise more than just student power.

The meeting concluded, Philip Clark drove his Mini

out of the pub car park and headed it back towards the College. 'No one's going to be sent down,' he said in answer to a question from Sarah who was sitting beside him. 'The wording is up to us, but it's pretty mild – and quite witty. Case of *honi soit* when you think about it.'

'You don't believe UCI is really going bust?'

'Of course not; colleges don't go bust. This one must be coining it. If they were in trouble they'd be running appeals, and putting up the fees. They're just greedy, that's all – greedy for the pig farm money. Well, that should be a thing of the past after tonight.' Philip swung the car into the college drive. 'I'm not sure there's anything in the Arab business in any case. Faisal's pretty tight about it. Anyway, if it comes to anything we deal with it later. Today's the day we rout the yokels.' He glanced at the girl, who appeared mollified. 'I don't mind carrying the can for the protest; it just doesn't compare with what goes on at some universities.'

'Sit-ins are boring.'

'Exactly – and infantile,' said Philip loftily, being privately thankful that no one had suggested holding one. 'You know,' he added thoughtfully, 'since we've got our fall-back position if there's real trouble – so has the college ... if there's a problem over funds, I mean. There's a hell of a lot more there than firework money – or so Roger says.'

The seating arrangements at lunch in the Senior Common Room had not taken the form that the Dean intended, but they suited Treasure admirably. He had succeeded in placing himself next to Dr Goldstein, who had made for the foot of the long, rectangular table while the voluble Ribble had been settling Mrs Hatch and Witaker to his own right and left at the other end. Miss Stopps was opposite Treasure, and Peter Gregory, the Australian to whom he had taken an instant liking, was on his other side. The banker was thus protected from further direct exposure to the Dean's rhetoric along several yards of polished oak, flanked by an assortment of faculty members.

While Witaker had been fairly subdued throughout the meal, Treasure had been amused to observe that Mrs Hatch had not been nearly so overwhelmed by Ribble. She had frequently talked the Dean down by the simple process of breaking in on him at greater volume. He, in turn, had assumed the lady was deaf, and at each new opportunity had increased his own bass response. The resulting dialogue had drowned any attempt at independent discourse for some two-thirds of the table length.

'Ribble is a noisy man, but his heart, as they say, is in the right place: I wonder sometimes about his brain. More coffee, Treasure?' Dr Goldstein delivered the judgement and the invitation without passion or emphasis. Treasure had earlier noted the mode of address, which implied a proper degree of familiarity without the unction that others present had been affording him.

'Thank you.' Treasure pushed his coffee cup towards the Senior Tutor. 'I have the impression that the Dean's heart and mind are probably here in this place.'

'Quite right, UCI would have collapsed around us all without his tireless – and sometimes tiresome – application. There are times when he shames me into an irritating consciousness of my own lack of vigour in the same cause.' Goldstein did not look particularly conscience-stricken, but he sounded sincere.

'The Senior Tutor is noted for his modesty, Mr Treasure,' put in Peter Gregory, and Treasure, not for the first time, registered the feeling that the breezy young Australian and the celebrated Dr Goldstein were on terms that licensed the junior man's easy relationship with the other. The compliment had in no way displeased Goldstein through the touch of sarcasm in its construction. 'In fact, we couldn't do without him either,' Gregory continued. 'He and the Dean make a pretty formidable pair when we're threatened from the outside. You might not guess it, but you'd better believe it . . . sir.'

Treasure smiled at the remembered civility. 'I get the impression you live in daily fear of being closed down.'

'Not daily; annual perhaps – and even that's an exaggeration.' This from Goldstein. 'We're something of an anachronism and one hell of an embarrassment to the red-brick brigade. It may sound precious, but in less than twenty years we've built a reputation for enthusiastic scholarship that's almost un-British. People come here to work, not to indulge in political posturing or to train for the Olympics – our sporting record is appalling. But then we're not trying to out-do Oxford and Cambridge – the scale is quite different, for one thing. We do what we're good at – and we do it very well.'

'But if you were bigger . . .'

'We'd be a hell of a sight worse, Mr Treasure,' Gregory interrupted. 'I've been offered better-paid jobs at bigger places but I'm certainly not ready to quit the atmosphere of UCI – not yet awhile, anyway.' The last comment came as a spoken reaction to the private and levelling thought that marriage to the daughter of a member of the Stock Exchange Council might produce responsibilities beyond the capacity of the speaker's current stipend.

Goldstein was less adamant. 'Some growth is desirable – even perhaps overdue, but it needs to be controlled growth. There's the problem. We're too late to hope for eventual university status – and the money that would go with it. So Whitehall and the other powers that control these things are not going to cough up piddling sums of money for odd additional faculties. Result, stalemate.'

'Or the Funny Farms Foundation?' Treasure spoke without emotion.

'Which would be disastrous – and I mean disastrous. You can have no concept of what this place stands for if you truly believe you can graft on such an absurdity.' Goldstein was clearly quite impervious to the offence he might be offering. 'Peter and I have opposed the idea from the very beginning. The thing is an academic obscenity, and it will happen over my dead body.'

'And after he's done in a few others for good measure,' Gregory added with a grin.

The bond between the Senior Tutor and the Reader in English Literature was evidently bedded in a cause as well as in mutual esteem. The vehemence and irritation in Goldstein's voice caused Treasure to change course. 'Extra money might be raised by appeal,' he offered. 'There is a Trust Fund. Indeed, I'm here partly to represent one of the three Trustees . . .'

'Who have no control over our destiny.' Goldstein was unmollified. 'You can't lumber us with obligations we don't want. The Trustees are a fund-raising body pure and simple – and the other two are both pure *and* simple; a bishop and the College lawyer. I've met your chap, Grenwood. None of them bothered to be here today, incidentally.'

'I wondered about the Bishop,' observed Treasure, determined not to be ruffled. 'Your lawyer couldn't make it today, I know; but the Bishop was supposed to be here.'

'He's been sick, I think, but getting better,' said Gregory, glad to follow through on a subject that was lowering the temperature. 'Miss Stopps might know.' He looked across the table towards the lady who appeared to be half engaged in conversation with the College Lecturer in European Cultural History. 'Do you know what the trouble was, Miss Stopps?' he asked, raising his voice.

'Syphilis – riddled with it,' came the surprising reply. 'Such a talent too. I suppose he got it from cohabiting with the natives in Tahiti. Are you also an admirer of the Impressionists, Mr Treasure?'

'We were discussing the Bishop, Miss Stopps,' said Gregory. 'Surely he hasn't got syphilis?'

'Good gracious, I hope not. Who could have told you such a thing?' Miss Stopps glanced around the others with an expression of real alarm. 'We were talking of Gauguin . . .'

The opportunity to clear the reputation of the maligned

Bishop was lost. The Dean stood up and was banging the table with a spoon. For a fleeting moment Treasure assumed this might represent some desperate last attempt on the part of Ribble to establish private conversational superiority over Mrs Hatch, but this was not the case. 'Ladies and gentlemen,' said the Dean loudly, 'in five minutes' time I propose to take our guests on a tour of the College. If those of you involved in our . . . er . . . our business meeting would be good enough to reassemble here at three o'clock . . .'

'Business meeting my foot,' said Goldstein to Treasure, in more than a stage whisper, as Ribble continued to speak. 'He's got twelve out of fifteen faculty members voting for your foul endowment and he's rigging what he thinks will be a demonstration of solidarity. Well, wait and see.'

'. . . so if the ladies would now like to retire? Miss Stopps?' Ribble looked down the table expectantly at Tottle's mistress, who rose to her feet, grasped her vast bag, and made to conduct Mrs Hatch away as it had evidently been arranged that she should. The one other lady present – the shy-looking Head of the Modern Languages Department – also left, but by a different door. Treasure guessed that Mrs Hatch and Miss Stopps were to have the exclusive use of whatever superior ablutionary facilities were available close by.

Remembering Goldstein's last comment, Treasure turned to him, as they both stood watching the ladies leave, and asked, 'Have the students been consulted about the Funny Farms project? I gather it's fashionable these days . . .'

'To have the lunatics running the asylums?' cut in Goldstein firmly. He smiled before continuing. 'Fortunately our lunatics are pretty well tamed or we wouldn't let them in. No, we don't go in for student participation in long-term decision-making, for the very good reason such things are not their concern. Unofficially I gather our young things would prefer not to be part of an agricultural college. But why don't you ask them?'

The double doors through which the two ladies had left were still open. Miss Stopps suddenly reappeared from the hall on the other side moving at a cracking pace and in a state of some agitation. She made for the Dean, but her opening exclamation was heard by everyone. 'Mr Dean, a most ill-conceived prank. I fear our visitor deserves the most abject apology . . . Extended between the taps of the hand basin . . .'

Before Miss Stopps could complete her report, attention was diverted by the appearance of Amelia Hatch. She held out before her a string threaded through eight severed chicken heads. She stood in the doorway, smiled wryly in Witaker's direction, and observed, 'As I keep saying, Irv, someone's tryin' to get a message through.'

CHAPTER VI

TREASURE REGARDED the retreating figure of Major Hunter-Smith for a moment before turning to begin a stroll along the lakeside. The Dean's business meeting was not due to begin for a further ten minutes, and the banker looked forward to some private contemplation after a crowded hour. He decided to inspect the little boat-house which lay some hundred yards along from where he had been talking with the Bursar on the steps of the Hall.

The persons most discommoded by the incident of the chicken heads – Ribble, Witaker and Miss Stopps – had been pacified by the individual least affected, namely Amelia Hatch. 'Lan' sakes, students will be students – and I can take a joke,' had been Amelia's good-humoured summary of the whole affair. Nevertheless, even a warning look from his client had not prevented Witaker from re-tailing the story of the sheep's head, which produced further expressions of outrage and sympathy.

Since he had not earlier mentioned the package sent to Lord Grenwood, Treasure might have chosen to do so then. On reflection, he chose to remain silent. He had not known about the sheep's head either until Witaker had recounted the story – obviously against the better judge-ment of Mrs Hatch. It was the lady's attitude to the two incidents that prompted him not to disclose the existence of a third – this despite the fact that each considerably enlarged the significance of the others. In Treasure's private opinion the triple demonstration was more elaborate and somehow more insidious than the usual product of student protest. The chicken heads had not been accompanied by a message but it was inconceivable that their existence had not been contrived by the same hand or hands as the other two sanguinary warnings.

Decorating the taps in the ladies' wash-room at the Hall involved considerably greater risk of discovery than delivering packages to hotels or merchant banks. The absence of an exhortation might simply relate to a shortage of time.

Treasure had dutifully accompanied the inspecting party on its tour of UCI and its amenities. He had been duly complimentary about the state of the kitchens, the abundance of lecture rooms, the comparative comfort of the student accommodation, and the immensity of the bathrooms. In turn, he had sympathized about the budget restrictions that limited the cuisine, the availability of books, the numbers of lecturers, the complement of students, and the occurrence of baths. Finally he had sagely regarded the acres of rolling parkland available for extra building – assuredly in harmonious style – and the nurture of whatever animals and crops that might prove consistent with the objects of the Funny Farms Faculty of Agriculture.

Witaker had been non-committal throughout the ramble. Mrs Hatch, in sharp contrast, had been ecstatically enthusiastic about the whole establishment. Her only expressed regret had been about the marked absence of students available for encounter. Treasure had noted the same fact. Young people could sometimes be observed in the far or middle distance but seemed to evaporate when the party approached. Ribble had explained that Friday afternoons inevitably produced an exodus of students with parental homes not too far distant – weekend exeats being available for the asking, a practice consistent with the need to save food, light and heat. He later seemed to discount this whole story by promising a huge attendance at the firework display and entreating Mrs Hatch to remain for the event. On balance, Treasure construed that students were avoiding the visitors and that the Dean knew it.

The tour had included an embarrassing interlude. The party had emerged from the north side of the Hall intent

on visiting the stable block at precisely the same moment
that Sheikh Al Haban and his retinue had appeared on
foot through the archway immediately opposite. The two
groups were separated by a ciruclar sward of grass skirted
by a wide gravel drive but also bisected north and south
by a path provided for those more concerned with
direct communication than with perambulation.

The Dean had immediately arrested the progress of his
own party with some credible but unnecessary com-
mentary about the view, while waiting to see which
direction was adopted by the Arab visitors. As a strategy
to avoid direct confrontation – and Treasure guessed it
was such – this had everything to commend it. Unfortunately, Al Haban was clearly of the same mind.
Both parties remained rooted in their territories for longer
than was consistent with whatever intention either had
invented for appearing in the first place.

It was Ribble who had made the first move by leading
the Funny Farms contingent to the right, but only
fractionally sooner than the Crown Prince also abandoned
indecision and led his entourage on a collision course to
his left. Before it was too late for either man to adopt an
opposite direction with minimum but still preserved
decorum, both did so. This caused a certain amount of
confusion in both camps. The Dean's violent about-turn
led him straight into the arms of Amelia Hatch who had
been following close behind. She, in turn, recoiled on to
Witaker so that all three had momentarily become
engaged in a curious *pas de trois* for ill-matched per-
formers.

Meantime, although Al Haban had turned about, he
had paused to motion aside his followers with a sweep of
his arm before actually embarking on a new course. This
had given him the opportunity to observe Ribble's change
of plan and to counter it by stepping directly on to the
grass, continuing in a southerly direction at the side of the
path that divided the lawn. Ribble, whose intended
progress had been effectively blocked by the Hatch-

Witaker ensemble, also stepped on to the grass on the opposite side of the path, and headed north.

Thus it was that, with opportunity for further dissembling well past, the two parties had approached each other in the style of army patrols, neither of them treading the six-foot-wide gravel pathway so obviously provided for their progress – and which thus took on the character of 'no-man's-land'. 'It is pleasant to walk upon grass,' remarked the Dean with an evident and justifiable lack of conviction: he had been responsible for the notices scattered about cautioning people to abjure precisely that pleasure.

'Makes you wanna toss your shoes off,' said Mrs Hatch in a tone that presaged intention more than it indicated idle observation.

Witaker had resigned himself to the thought that this was exactly the kind of peasant-like compulsion to which his client would abandon herself some seconds before encountering a Middle Eastern potentate. Treasure, who was bringing up the rear with Major Hunter-Smith, had speculated on the possibility of that same potentate finding himself bombarded with tossed shoes.

'Good afternoon, your Royal Highness.' Ribble had halted where the two groups had drawn abreast, and gave a stiff little bow. Amelia, not to be outdone, lined herself up beside the Dean, dropped a deep, wobbly curtsey, and fell over. Witaker, wishing he were somewhere else – anywhere else – had helped her to regain her feet.

Amelia had lost her balance, but not her composure. 'Sorry about that, your Regal Highness,' she hollered across the path that still divided the parties. She smiled warmly at Al Haban, then, after a frankly appraising glance, she added, 'Gee, you look swell in those duds.' An honest observation which Treasure felt neutralized the suggestion of overdone deference in the curtsey.

Al Haban had shown neither pleasure nor displeasure at the confrontation. The Dean had mumbled introductions while the two groups remained incongruously

planted on either side of the path – a situation which at
least precluded any question of hand-shaking. The
Sheikh – his gaze resting upon Treasure – had formally
presented his son, but ignored the presence of his two
retainers who had taken up positions behind him.

It was not until the two groups had moved on in their
separate directions that Treasure was stopped by a gentle
voice from behind. 'Excuse me, sir.' It was young Prince
Faisal. 'My father would be honoured if you would take
tea with us at four-thirty.'

Treasure had smiled at the young man and then in the
direction of Sheikh Al Haban who had stopped, looking
his way, some yards distant. The older men bowed
slightly to each other as the banker had replied, 'Please
tell your father I am more than honoured to be invited.
Until four-thirty then, Prince Faisal.'

Only Hunter-Smith had overheard this exchange, and
he had made no comment upon it. Indeed, the Bursar had
seemed preternaturally concerned to concentrate his and
Treasure's whole attention on a not very subtle examination of the reasons why University College might, after all,
be unworthy of the Funny Farms endowment. At first,
Treasure had taken the view that this was evidence of
extreme objectivity on the part of the Bursar, who had
been author of the College's first application for the
money. Since, however, the diatribe had continued
throughout the tour, and even after it was over, Treasure
found himself more puzzled to know what prompted it
than he was influenced by its content.

The Dean had taken great pride in showing off the
Stable Quadrangle, remarking particularly on the way in
which the attic storey – added only twenty years before –
harmonized with the original Georgian. Certain in the
knowledge that the whole Arab party was engaged elsewhere, he confidently invited Treasure and the Americans
into Prince Faisal's set of rooms, and in a distinctly
proprietorial manner. That this was more assumed than
justified became obvious when the style of furnishing was

compared with that in Peter Gregory's rooms opposite, and which the party had examined just before – also in the absence of the tenant.

Gregory's material comforts had been distinctly of the institutional variety – adequate but ordinary. The Prince, on the other hand, clearly lived in a style suited to his station. As an undergraduate at Oxford, Treasure had not been wealthy enough to do more than add a few wall prints in an attempt to stamp his own personality on the group of not very well-matched chattels provided in his College rooms. He had envied those few of his contemporaries who could afford to dispense with College furniture and bring their own from home or Harrods. Prince Faisal had evidently been able to go one further by inviting an interior designer with a great deal of taste, and a long budget, to create an atmosphere conducive to both relaxation and study.

The arrangements and the fittings were almost wholly western and modern. Treasure noted and approved some chairs recognizably by Charles Eames, and a desk he guessed had been designed by Clive Hunt. The single marked concession to the owner's origins was in the decoration of one wall. Above a low, long bookcase that ran the length of the sitting-room on one side there hung a variety of Arabian utensils and weaponry, mostly with gold or beaten silver ornamentation. In the centre was a truly handsome collection of swords, scimitars and daggers in delicately-worked scabbards. Amelia Hatch had been fascinated by this display and took down several pieces to examine them more closely.

Treasure, mindful of his appointment later in these same rooms, and of the fact that the party was present in them uninvited, had quietly slipped away down the stairs and into the quadrangle where he had waited, near the empty Cadillac, for the others to complete their inspection of the Prince's possessions. This action was prompted partly by the feeling that he was trespassing – despite the presence of the Dean – but more because it would be embarrassing for all – and especially for him – to be found trespassing through the untimely return of Sheikh Al Haban. Thus Treasure had no means of telling, later, which member of the party it had been who left the rooms last.

The remainder of the tour had been uneventful. The Dean and his companions had run into Miss Stopps – almost literally – when she turned into the stable entrance, moving well, with head leading, and right shoulder down, at the same moment that they were emerging from the pilastered opening. She had earlier excused herself from accompanying Mrs Hatch on the journey around the College. Since lunch she had been to her cottage a mile away in the village, fed Tottle, provided herself with warmer clothing in preparation for attendance at the firework display, and returned by car. So much was evident or announced. Treasure could discern little difference in the lady's appearance, save for a slight increase in overall bulk. Tottle was not visible, but Miss Stopps's unexpected conveyance – a red Triumph Stag 3-litre convertible – had been neatly parked nearby. Apart from being amused by the incongruity of the vehicle in relation to its owner, Treasure had wondered which insurance company found the two acceptable as a risk.

Miss Stopps had assured the Dean that she would be present for his meeting half an hour later, but declared that she had to call on Peter Gregory meantime. Nor was she deterred by the intelligence that Gregory was out; she had prepared a note to leave against this very eventuality.

It was Miss Stopps that Treasure and Hunter-Smith had been discussing just before they had parted. The banker had understood earlier that Miss Stopps had been formally involved in the day's events as proxy for the Bishop – the ailing Trustee she had inadvertently maligned. From what the Bursar said, however, it became apparent that the lady certainly owned a moral right of her own to a voice in the planning of the College's future.

Treasure was astonished to learn that Miss Stopps

made an annual covenanted donation of ten thousand
pounds to the UCI Trust Fund. He was as much surprised
at the earnest this offered of affluence as at the generosity
involved. Hunter-Smith had gone on to say that there had
been hints of an eventual, substantial legacy for the
College from the same source, that Miss Stopps was tireless in her devotion to the institution, roundly against the
Funny Farms project, and rich enough to secure the
financial security of UCI by herself, possibly in her lifetime and certainly at the end of it – always provided, the
Bursar had cautioned darkly, that she was not upset.

In view of Hunter-Smith's obvious change of heart over
the acceptability of the Funny Farms money, Treasure
had allowed for a degree of subjectivity in this report. He
was still curious to know more about the background of
Miss Stopps and what it was that prompted her very real
affection for the College. He had already worked out –
almost as a reflex thought process – that if Miss Stopps's
income was generated by capital, assuming her living
expenses were modest – a point not reflected by her choice
of car, but allowing for occasional extravagances – her
fortune could be hardly less than a quarter of a million
pounds. Further, if Miss Stopps ran true to form with
other elderly ladies of her type with whom Treasure was
acquainted, the sum might be even larger – considerably
larger.

The Bursar was less clear about Miss Stopps's provenance than Treasure might have hoped. He knew that her
father had been 'in trade' in the area – probably Southampton. The Major had delivered the occupational ap-
pellation in a tone that suggested his own background lay
in higher social spheres: Hunter-Smith worked hard to
suggest he had been the younger son of faded gentry put
to the Colours in defence of the Empire. In fact his father
had been a respectable harbour master at an east coast
port – just defensibly not in trade.

Miss Stopps, despite her reputedly humble origins, had
owned some connection or friendship with the last family

to occupy the Hall. More than this the Bursar could not offer, save that she had lived in the village since well before the war, and had certainly been involved with UCI since its inception. 'Dashed poor show if the dear lady is made to feel excluded by this American business. I'd hate to feel responsible for that.' This statement, intended to sound bluff and honest, had been Hunter-Smith's parting shot before leaving Treasure to prepare for the meeting.

The banker strolled along the water's edge, stopped for a moment to glance at the deserted but unfinished scaffolding for the fireworks, wondered why such complicated arrangements were necessary, and continued on towards the boat-house.

Despite the urging of Lord Grenwood, Treasure had heard and seen enough now to have considerable doubts about the propriety of the Funny Farms Foundation adopting UCI. It was clear that the American endowment would represent far more than the College's current income, and thus that it might become the tail that wagged the dog. There appeared to be a strong and influential body of opinion against the proposal – led by Dr Goldstein, who certainly had the best intellect in the College. The views of Peter Gregory and the Bursar in the same context rated consideration for different reasons – though Treasure had to admit still to not understanding the Bursar's change of heart. If Miss Stopps, the benefactor, would truly be upset by the acceptance of the endowment, then, in view of her present and future importance to the institution's financial standing, her attitude gave pause for thought.

Treasure found it surprising that Miss Stopps had not made her opposition plain to him when there had been several opportunities for her to do so. This train of thought reminded him that it had been Miss Stopps who had first alerted him to the possibility of an Arab 'take-over'. Surmise about this eventuality would doubtless be replaced by hard fact over tea in Prince Faisal's rooms.

The more Treasure thought about it, the more it appeared to him that the College could do without the conditional endowment in Mrs Hatch's gift which, if accepted, had to mean a fundamental alteration in the character of the place. What appeared to be needed was a modest improvement in capital or income. Several ideas went through Treasure's mind. He excluded the notion of a sell-out to Al Haban, but he saw the possibility of a compromise solution with the Arabs. At the same time he felt obliged to caution himself into remembering the purpose of his visit. Such schemes as he had in mind hardly fitted him in his role as adviser to Amelia Hatch, nor did they even fulfil the express wishes of Lord Grenwood.

'Hands up, or I fire.'

Treasure was jerked back to reality by this stern directive. It was issued by a youth of about twenty who had suddenly got up from the bottom of a punt moored at the boat-house from where he had been watching the banker's progress unobserved. The boy was dressed in khaki overalls; his head was uncovered and completely bald – a feature that lent his unlined face a strangely aged appearance. His legs were wide apart, and both arms were stretched out before him. His hands were clasped around a frighteningly large automatic pistol, pointed directly at Treasure.

'Put the gun down, you young fool,' exclaimed Treasure, sounding more courageous than he felt.

'I warned you,' answered the boy – and pulled the trigger.

CHAPTER VII

TREASURE PICKED himself up from where he had dived on to the ground, and to the accompaniment of peals of laughter from the youth who had jumped ashore and was skipping towards his erstwhile victim. He waved the gun above his head so that the silk banner which had unfolded from beneath the barrel was clearly visible, as was the word 'Bang' inscribed upon it.

Viewed from close quarters, the 'pistol' was obviously an elaborate toy. At ten yards, and to a man whose eyesight was marginally – but only marginally – less than perfect, it had looked like the real thing. The prank had been foolhardy. One read of men of Treasure's age – indeed, of men a good deal younger – who suffered severe coronary effects as a result of such shocks. Nor were the repercussions always evident at the time; they could be cumulative. Probably the dive would have been pointless if the gun had been real – but it had been well executed. There was a grass stain on the left elbow of the dog's-tooth check – and the joint was a bit painful. Damn the fellow.

Treasure felt angry and foolish. 'You realize that was an extremely stupid thing to do. I've half a mind to punch your head in.' The lad was quite frail. 'As it is, I shall certainly report you to the Dean. What's your name?'

The boy had stopped laughing. He stared at Treasure in evident disbelief. Then his expression changed to one of acute sadness. A tear coursed down one cheek. The slight body began to heave with silent sobbing.

Treasure had reduced a grown youth to tears. 'Oh, for God's sake pull yourself together,' he said, now more embarrassed than angry: the lachrymose reaction was disarmingly unexpected.

The boy lifted his bald head which Treasure noticed

was traced diagonally by an ugly scar. He could see too that one part of the scalp was truly hairless, while the remainder was shaven. The expression on the boy's face was now so pathetically full of remorse that Treasure found himself growing sorry for the wretched fellow.

'Please don't tell on me, sir. Please don't tell. I won't do it again, I promise. You can have the gun – Auntie gave it to me, and I promised her I wouldn't . . . Oh, *please* don't tell Auntie.' The tears were now rolling down the pale cheeks.

Treasure was sure that the performance was genuine; what he found difficult to credit was that it was being played by a young adult and not a ten-year-old. He and his wife had lost their only child, a boy, at that last age, and the conduct of the frail creature before him was bitingly reminiscent of a dozen similar scenes played by that other, sad, anaemic child when half the age of this one.

The sympathy Treasure was feeling deepened into understanding. 'You're not an undergraduate . . . a student here, are you?'

'No, sir . . . I'm Andy, sir . . . I'm guard of the fireworks, sir. Auntie said I could stay if I was good . . . and the others said I could help. Oh please, sir, don't tell them I've been naughty.'

'Where do you live, Andy?'

'In the village, sir . . . with Auntie . . . You're not going to send me home, are you, sir? Oh, please let me stay.'

Treasure heard voices behind him. He glanced over his shoulder: Amelia Hatch and Witaker were approaching from the Hall. 'All right, Andy, I'll let you off this time, but you must promise never to frighten anyone with that thing again.' He smiled gently at the boy. 'Now cut along back to the punt . . . and, er, and keep guard.' Treasure caught himself falling into the role of prep school master. Andy bolted towards the boat-house.

'Good Gard, did you see that kid?' Amelia looked and sounded more astonished than the sight of Andy's dis-

figurement should decently have prompted in a person
with normal sensitivities. Her exclamation had been
addressed to Witaker; he appeared not to have noticed the
boy who was now some distance away.

'A case of arrested development, I think,' said Treasure
quietly, 'possibly caused by an accident. A rather pathetic
case.' This last remark was intended as a mild reproof.

Mrs Hatch paused uncertainly for a moment; then she
gazed after Andy. 'Poor guy. Gee, I'm sorry. Does he
work here?'

'I doubt it,' replied Treasure, mollified. 'He lives with
an aunt in the village. Were you looking for me?'

'Only that it's time for the meeting, Mr Treasure. Me
and Irv were wondering if we should take up a party line.'

The three turned towards the Hall.

'We have not, as you keep insisting, reached a stalemate,
Dean.' Goldstein was formal, precise, and angry. 'It is
quite plain that a majority of the Governing Body and
the resident staff are in favour of your proposition, as is
this . . . this lady and her advisers.' He nodded towards
Mrs Hatch, as though the classification required con-
firming. 'It is equally plain to me that you are ready to
write off the tradition and the record of this place for the
paltry reason that we are in need of money – apparently
from any source and on any conditions. There is no stalemate; you intend to sell out.'

The speaker leaned back in his chair, folded his arms,
and stared sternly ahead of him – which, as it happened,
meant that Treasure who was sitting opposite became the
undeserving object of a thoroughly disaffected glare.

'In fairness to our guests, the source of the money is
impeccable, and the conditions entirely to do with
academics.' Ribble spoke from the head of the table. 'This
is, after all, an educational establishment and it's entirely
reasonable . . .'

'That we should turn it into a training school for milk-
maids and cowboys. You're surely not suggesting that

what's proposed would even allow us to conduct normal degree courses in agriculture?'

Treasure looked to Witaker in expectation of some comment, but since the lawyer made none, he put in himself; 'I understood, Dr Goldstein, that you'd all been made aware the Foundation has no objection to funding first degree courses in conventional agriculture, provided the post-graduate school is devoted to pure food projects and research.'

'Quite right,' said Ribble. 'As Dean, I insisted on that point being cleared at the early stages. Indeed, we have the Bursar to thank for producing the workable formula that has made our negotiations possible.' He smiled warmly at Hunter-Smith, who sincerely hoped the compliment would never be repeated in the presence of his wife.

'We are still having to incorporate certain safeguards . . .'

'Aw, shucks to safeguards.' Amelia Hatch interrupted Witaker loudly. 'We bin touting this proposition long enough to know where the problems lie, an' I guess we've gotten smart enough to find ways around 'em. What Mr Treasure says is right. Mr Hatch would have seen the sense of it – why, he was the mos' practical man you ever met. Ain't that so, Irv?'

Witaker did not find it necessary to do more than nod a bare assent to this tacit admission that what Cyrus Hatch had originally envisioned was wholly impractical, not to say demonstrably cuckoo. Treasure had already divined that Mrs Hatch was resigned to compromise if dedicated to establishing the Funny Farms Faculty of Agriculture at all costs, rather than have to admit failure, and, with it, her late husband's asinine whimsicality.

'Might I ask?' The six others present, including Dr Goldstein, looked towards Miss Stopps who was making her first contribution since the start of the hour-long meeting. 'Might I ask, does the endowment have to be for ever? It seems, as it were, such a very long time – I mean such a very permanent commitment.'

'I'm afraid that is the central condition, Dean,' said Witaker, addressing the Chairman and producing the words with great emphasis. 'The fact that some employment of the Foundation's capital is to be permitted during the first five years – to provide new buildings and so on – puts a legal as well as a moral obligation on the College to follow through with the project on a permanent basis.'

'But, as I understand it, it's intended that the capital should be made up again out of income over the following twenty years.' This came from Treasure. 'Also, the American Trustees of the Foundation can withhold the endowment at any time after the fifth year either on a temporary or permanent basis.'

'By which time the College will own a whole string of new buildings, Mr Treasure, put up at our expense – we ain't gonna abandon that kind of stake without good reason.' Treasure had to agree with Amelia's argument.

'One might then regard the first five years as an experimental period?' asked Miss Stopps with more than a note of hope in her voice: Treasure had an informed guess at the special reason for her question.

'Oh, nothing so loose, I'm afraid,' said Witaker, again with firmness. 'The Trustees would only withdraw their support if totally dissatisfied with the way the Faculty was run. In view of some of the conditions applying to the curriculum – the appointment to fellowships and so on – I really can't see the circumstances ever arising.'

Treasure wished he could feel that Witaker intended to sound reassuring; in fact, what the lawyer had said had been delivered in tones that suggested a threat.

'In short, the bondage is going to be permanent.' Goldstein was not mincing words – or deeds. He stood up. 'If this arrangement goes through I shall exert all the influence in my power to ensure that degrees in agriculture cannot be awarded through this College. *That* should provide your Foundation with adequate grounds for dissatisfaction, madam. I shall also resign my position here. Good afternoon.'

The Senior Tutor's angry departure was followed by an embarrassed silence. The Dean treated the others to a sickly smile that was meant to inspire confidence. 'High spirits,' he said, 'nothing more than a display of high spirits, I assure you.' A remark that Treasure considered might constitute the most dangerous understatement he had heard in several months. Equally, however, in view of Goldstein's comments during lunch, he had found the Senior Tutor's expostulations and threats somehow less unnerving and damaging that he had been led to expect.

'Can he wreck the deal, Dean?' Mrs Hatch was characteristically direct.

'Certainly not,' replied Ribble firmly. 'The Senior Tutor's relationship with our degree-awarding authority is remote; they may note any protest he makes, but I happen to know they won't act upon it.'

'And Dr Goldstein's resignation?' Miss Stopps sounded anxious.

'Is unlikely to materialize.' On this point Ribble seemed more than confident. 'Daniel Goldstein threatens to resign over some issue or other almost annually – last term because we proposed putting up student fees – but as you see, he's still here.'

'We didn't put up the fees, Dean,' offered Hunter-Smith.

'Technically, no we didn't.' Ribble still appeared sure of his ground. 'We made some economies, and thanks to a most generous gift – an anonymous gift – we expect to balance the books.'

'Even so, Dean, as a Trustee of the Foundation, and its legal counsellor, I need absolute assurance . . .'

'And I can give you just that, Mr Witaker, oh dear me, yes,' Ribble interrupted. 'An overwhelming majority of the Governing Body plus a substantial majority of the Faculty are in favour of accepting the endowment. It's only natural, even in an establishment as relatively small as this one, that there should be some dissentient voices to a

proposition as . . . er . . . original as the one you are
making. In general, however, I can promise you we shall
fulfil our obligations in the spirit as well as the letter.'

'And that's good enough for me and Irv,' said Amelia,
with a meaningful glance directed at Witaker – but one
which he chose to disregard.

'I ought to tell you,' said the lawyer, 'in view of the
opposition that's been expressed, we received another
application this morning from another apparently respectable establishment. We intended to disregard it, but I
guess now we may need to consider it.'

Ribble looked surprised. 'Might I ask the name of the
establishment?'

'The Torchester Polytechnic. They already have a
school of agriculture but they want to enlarge it. The
conditions they propose are pretty well identical to the
ones you put up.' The Bursar was suddenly overwhelmed
with a coughing fit which resulted in his becoming
extremely red in the face as Witaker continued. 'Mr
Treasure agrees that Torchester would normally deserve
consideration.'

'I certainly think it's a candidate,' said Treasure with
emphasis on the last word. He was anxious to sound
impartial, and in any case, he hardly knew the place.

'Oh, most respectable,' put in Miss Stopps, implying a
surprisingly intimate knowledge of educational facilities in
the far north of England. 'I believe you might be well
advised to investigate its potential, Mrs Hatch.'

Ribble smiled confidently. 'They've got over their left-
wing troubles, then?'

'Left-wing troubles? Jeepers, are they a bunch of
Commies?' demanded Mrs Hatch, quickly transformed
into a predictably outraged, if repentant, daughter of an
eighteenth-century revolution.

'International Socialists, I believe,' responded Ribble,
as though the point were academic. Treasure remembered
the events – two years earlier – that had provided the
Dean with his telling and well-timed observation. Tor-

chester, like a number of other similar establishments, had been subject to a wave of student rioting. Dissatisfaction with the size of student grants had been channelled into political disaffection. A mood of normal unrest had long since replaced the turmoil that had been short-lived; the facts were nevertheless undeniable.

'That settles it,' said Amelia, 'we ain't backing any Reds, and that's for sure. Why, one of the fine things I bin told about Itchendever is the way you've avoided any such nonsense.'

'The undergraduates here are extremely sensible and well-behaved.' It was Miss Stopps who volunteered the confirmation. Treasure found her gratuitous offering surprising until her following remark. 'It remains to be seen, of course, whether they will welcome the Funny Farms Faculty of Agriculture.' Miss Stopps gave full emphasis to the alliterative aspect of the name, in a manner that gave maximum advertisement to its comic quality.

'Ah yes, students come and go, of course.' Ribble stated the obvious as though it were the essence of profundity. 'In three years there will be few in residence who will have known Itchendever without its illustrious new appendage.' Treasure found the description a trifle strong, but the presumption was nicely gauged.

'I guess we can leave the kids out of this.' Mrs Hatch had long since taken the view that student democracy was something you put down. 'Dean, we've made up our minds.' This time the glare directed at Witaker could only be interpreted one way. 'Mr Treasure said yesterday we'd be impressed, and we are. I'm sorry about Dr Goldstein, and I sure wish Miss Stopps here was a crack more enthusiastic about the deal – but maybe you'll come round in time, dear. What I mean to say is, we're goin' ahead. Irv here has a fancy agreement of intent all ready and he can get with your lawyers again tomorrow for the signing.' She paused to glance around the table. 'I just want you all to know, I'm tickled to death about the whole thing.'

CHAPTER VIII

TREASURE DEPLORED the decreasing importance and observance attaching to afternoon tea as a national institution. He had been known to suffer attendance at village fetes for the compensation of savouring home-made rock cakes. Golf clubs he was inclined to judge, at least in winter, more by the standards of the buttered toast than by the condition of the fairways. If obliged to visit an academic or an ecclesiastic, he tried always to do so at tea-time. Lunch *en famille* with a Vice Chancellor or a Bishop was rarely a culinary delight; tea, in the tradition of things, could be quite a different matter. He frequently recalled some truly outstanding Scotch pancakes appropriately provided by the waggish Dean of St Paul's following the memorial service to an Irish banker of Jewish descent.

It had thus been a wrench to leave the Senior Common Room at the point where Miss Stopps had been supervising the preparations for a serious tea. Treasure had actually seen a plate of cress sandwiches; there was mention too of cherry cake – a rapture unforeseen which might better have remained so since Treasure was not destined to consume any. The collation had been timed for four-thirty to suit Ribble who had hurried out after the meeting upon some evidently urgent occasion. Since Treasure was due to call upon Sheikh Al Haban at the half-hour there had seemed no purpose in hanging about: it would hardly have been seemly to start stuffing himself with sandwiches and cake unilaterally, and in a standing position, when it was clearly Miss Stopps's instruction and intention literally to serve tea around the SCR table, and at the appointed time.

Finding himself in the Stable Quadrangle some few minutes early for his appointment, Treasure had lit a pipe

and ambled around the square. Although some distance
from the staircase shared by Peter Gregory and Prince
Faisal, he could not fail to deduce that the noise of a
loudly slammed door had come from that same opening.
There was also the following clatter of footsteps descending the uncovered wooden steps. Treasure was approaching from the north when the Dean had emerged and
turned south looking ruffled and perturbed. He had
marched off in the direction of the Hall without noticing
Treasure. Whatever had upset Ribble, at least he was
returning to the consolation of cherry cake – or such was
the thought in Treasure's mind as, after glancing at his
watch, he had knocked out his pipe, and climbed the
steps to the Prince's rooms.

'My dear Mr Treasure, it was good of you to come. My
son will give us some tea, then I hope you can make the
time for a private chat. Is that chair quite comfortable?'
Sheikh Al Haban was all amiability, and without some of
the trappings that at first sight had made him look fear-
some and unapproachably dignified. The two retainers
were not in evidence. The Sheikh was bare-headed. The
moustache which had earlier accentuated its owner's air
of Eastern superiority now, in conjunction with a balding
pate and the neck-high white robe, helped give him the
appearance of a mild and middle-aged altar-server pre-
paring for Holy Communion.

'You will perhaps enjoy some of this delectable cake;
we get it from your Fortnum and Mason's. The tea is a
blend I have made up at the same store. A splendid
habit, the English tea-time.'

Treasure was warming to his host by the second. Al
Haban spoke English slowly and with a just detectable
effort; there was a trace, too, of American accent and
idiom. The young Prince, having provided the two men
with tea and cake, picked up some books and excused
himself on the pretext of visiting the library.

'I fear I have angered the Dean – though that was not
my intention.' Al Haban smiled good-naturedly before

continuing. 'He perhaps thinks I have been . . . er . . . taking him for a ride. In truth I believe I am more justified in thinking it is he who has been doing the driving.'

'I'm afraid I don't follow, Your Highness.' In the case of Arab dignitaries Treasure invariably carried lack of presumption to extremes.

'You don't know of my negotiations with Mr Ribble?'

'He hasn't raised the subject,' Treasure answered truthfully.

Al Haban studied Treasure for a moment, then nodded as though to affirm to himself the rightness of some decision. 'So, I will tell you. But first it is necessary that I acquaint you with some detail of my personal position.'

'As you please, Your Highness. You know I am a merchant banker?'

'The Vice-Chairman of Grenwood, Phipps who do not advise my family in this country. Is that what you were going to say?' Treasure smiled assent. 'Have no fear that I shall compromise through . . . lack of professional etiquette, Mr Treasure. Our meeting here today is fortuitous but not coincidental. I desire to own this College. You represent an American commercial interest with a similar aim. It is proper that we should talk. Should your Americans fail in their object you would, I think, be free to represent me here . . . and in other ways.'

Treasure had the uncomfortable feeling that he had just been offered a bribe; the discomfort was not, however, acute. Al Haban was probably aware that the Funny Farms business was an *ad hoc* assignment for Grenwood, Phipps, and one that could hardly compare with the prospect of handling his own family's financial affairs on an enduring basis. The American bank that served the Emir of Abu B'yat had no London office of its own. If Al Haban's family were having a change of heart in their attitude to Britain, then Grenwood, Phipps would be happy to be of immediate service; though not in the matter of University College, Itchendever.

'This is most interesting, Your Highness. I doubt you could buy this College – it's controlled by a complicated charitable Trust. Mrs Hatch isn't trying to buy it; she wants to endow it – and it looks as though she's succeeded. I've just come from a meeting . . .'

'Where this lady agreed to give her million dollars a year to Itchendever. Mr Treasure, that is over double the College's present income. She has bought the institution.'

'I see what you mean, certainly, but really these things don't work quite that way. The College Trustees, and the Governing Body – they make pretty effective buffers against outside influences – no matter how powerful.'

Al Haban appeared not to be impressed. 'Six months ago, Mr Treasure, I was led to understand that, in return for a gift of one million pounds, my family or its representatives would be permitted a majority of seats on the Board of Trustees. That too, I agree, would not give us ownership of the College – only control of it.'

Treasure laughed aloud. 'I agree the distinction is slim.'

'It is not our intention to exert undue influence. For myself I simply require places for my sons.'

'How many sons do you have?'

'Sixteen; I have been well blessed. But there are other considerations. My brothers, too, have sons.' Treasure decided not to enquire after the number of brothers or their progeny, but calculated that UCI might be hard pressed to accommodate all comers from the ruling house of Abu B'yat if the blessing had been universal. 'The education here is good,' the Sheikh continued. 'Frivolity and useless sport are not encouraged – we are a devout family.'

'Knowing your family's connections with the USA, I am a little surprised . . .'

'That we do not send our children there, Mr Treasure? We are not so enamoured with America as in time past. My father, the Emir, is – how do you say? – disenchanted with some aspects of American policy.'

'How is His Majesty?' Treasure enquired politely while thinking about something quite different.

'He doesn't like me.'

'I beg your pardon?'

'You heard correctly, and we speak in confidence. I am out of favour with my father – a shameful circumstance for one of my race and position, Mr Treasure. I have displeased my father, and so I labour to regain his favour. To control a British University will please him.'

'Itchendever is not quite a university, Your Highness; just a college.'

'Now it is you who make the fine distinctions, my friend. Degrees are awarded to students here. If numbers increase, university status would be conferred.'

Treasure was disinclined to argue the point. 'Was it the Dean who made you the offer in the summer? I must say, I doubt he was entitled.'

'Quite so; now, I doubt it too. At that time, however, the College was seriously short of funds. I believe the Dean was counting on a near-bankrupt situation to force the acceptance of my . . . my rescue bid.'

'Since we are speaking in confidence, Your Highness, were you perhaps responsible for an anonymous gift used to tide the College over into the present academic year?'

Al Haban looked perplexed. 'I know of no such gift. I have just been informed, however, by the Dean himself, that it will not be necessary – as he put it – for me to make so large a contribution as I had offered. At the same time, it will not be . . . er, it will not be appropriate for my family to be given more than one seat on the Board of Trustees.'

'And the number of places available to students from Abu B'yat will be strictly limited?'

'You are very perceptive, Mr Treasure. That is precisely the situation. It is suggested that I donate a quarter of a million pounds to the College Trust. In return, twenty-five student places will be guaranteed for ten

years.' Al Haban paused to utter a short sigh. 'The Dean
is requiring the penny and the bun, but this is not serving
my purpose. More cake, Mr Treasure?'

The banker helped himself to a third slice of Fortnum's
Rich Madeira. 'The Funny Farms endowment plus your
gift would, of course, put the College on a very firm
financial footing. Control would effectively remain with
those who hold it now. Quite a neat arrangement if it
comes off. But I suppose you're not inclined to co-
operate?' Treasure recalled the Dean's ruffled expression
when he had seen him leave the quadrangle earlier.

'I find the proposition quite preposterous, Mr Treasure
– it is also presumptuous. Understand, I am not easily
insulted.' The Sheikh stood up and began walking around
the room. 'I do not easily take offence,' he continued,
giving the appearance still of a white-robed acolyte, but
one who had mislaid the offertory plate. 'My offer was
generous. I understood it was accepted . . . oh, it was clear
there would be formalities, that the Dean would need to
gain the approval of his colleagues. But he had given me
his word. Is not the word of an Englishman still his bond,
Mr Treasure?'

There were occasions when Treasure reflected that this
particular aphorism featured more often as a personal
liability than a national asset. 'Mm,' he murmured,
examining the pipe – always a prop to sagacity – that he
had just produced from his pocket. 'An academic less
familiar with financial transactions than, for instance, you
or I, Your Highness, may perhaps be forgiven for allowing enthusiasm to cloud prudence and good judgement.'

Al Haban flashed a look at Treasure implying that if
the compliment was noted the pompous apologia left
something to be desired. 'So; we make allowances for Mr
Ribble, but I do not accept his new propostion – even
assuming he is entitled to make it. I have said so. This
caused him to be uneasy. Am I correct to assume that the
American deal is not quite done?'

'The formal part still has to be completed, Your Highness. D'you mind if I smoke?' Al Haban smiled and nodded. 'Mrs Hatch, whom you met briefly, has given her word . . .'

'And her word is her bond.' The Sheikh sounded bitter. He stopped pacing about and slumped into the chair opposite Treasure. 'I have promised to speak with the Dean – and perhaps Mrs Hatch – here later, after the display of fireworks. It would be most helpful if you were present.'

'Delighted, Your Highness.' There seemed no way of avoiding the fireworks short of praying for rain. 'I ought to warn you, though, that I don't see the Funny Farms Foundation endowing a College controlled from outside this country – that is if you're still of a mind to press for acceptance of your first offer.'

'Mr Treasure, I have no choice in the matter. I have told my father we shall own this College. Mr Ribble may believe he can go back on his word to me. I cannot break my word to my father.' Al Haban fixed Treasure with a gaze so intense as to be disturbing as well as uncomfortable. He continued in a quiet, earnest tone. 'Indeed, Mr Treasure, I will not break my word to my father – it is a matter of honour. A way must be found.' He paused before adding, 'Come in, my son, we are finished with our private conversation.'

Treasure had been sitting with his back to the doorway. He glanced over his shoulder to see Prince Faisal standing at the threshold; he had no way of telling how long the young man had been there.

News travels fast in closed communities. As soon as the College menial employed to transport the first plate of cress sandwiches to the SCR had acquitted herself of that instructive duty, numerous interested persons not present at the meeting were better informed on its alleged proceedings than some who had taken part in it.

Philip Clark, the President of the JCR, adjusted the folds of his karate-style bathrobe and, bare-legged,

struck his Bonnie-Prince-Charlie-before-Culloden pose on
the threadbare rug in his room. 'The Funny Farms business is bad enough, but to be taken over by Torchester
Poly in the process is the bloody end.'

'The absolute terminus,' agreed Sarah Green from the
bed where the only vestment handy for adjustment was
the top sheet, now decorously wrapped around her torso
in deference to the arrival of Roger Dribdon.

'That's only intelligent conjecture, mark you,' said the
JCR Secretary, who was reading for a law degree, 'but it's
pretty easy to see the way their minds are working.'

'Right, Roger; plan A with the thunder-flashes –
agreed?' said Philip from the command position in front
of a wall poster depicting a well-endowed female urging
all and sundry to 'Join the Lamb's Navy'.

'Yes – all laid on,' replied Roger in a tone markedly less
belligerent. 'If you'll just put your signature on these
minutes, that'll make it official.'

Daniel Goldstein, who had a home and a wife to return to
close by, continued to eschew both. Since storming out of
the meeting an hour before, he had shut himself away in
the College study where he gave tutorials. The room was
sparsely furnished, but he kept a record-player there.
Solitude and Bach invariably provided the best therapy
for his troubled mind. Point and counterpoint – the
essence of classical music and balanced thinking – were
working to a resolution; specifically in the Fourth
Brandenburg; with help, in the affairs of the College.
There were two distinguishable enemies, inimical to one
another as well as to the best interests of UCI – and there
lay the solution he sought.

It took a classically disciplined mind to order battle
between romantic antagonists; unsuspecting barbarians
might make a better description. Consciously he sought
and recited Burke's definition – 'whatsoever is fitted in any
sort to excite the ideas of pain and danger, that is to say,
whatever is in any sort terrible, is a source of the sublime.'

Yes, the licence in the phrases was admirably apposite.

Reginald Hunter-Smith sat at his desk in the Bursar's
Office, closed one eye, and poured himself another stiff
whisky. So long as all the liquid went in the glass he knew
he was sober enought to drink it. In any case what he had
consumed at the bun-fight provided a solid enough base
for at least two more tots. Damn all women – especially
Mrs Hatch and his own lady wife. Gradually the fear of
going home was being stifled by the resolution that he was
not going home – not for a bit anyway.

He stared at himself in the hand-mirror kept in the
centre drawer. 'Hunter-Smith,' he said aloud, then
looked hurriedly around the room to ensure he was still
alone; this gave him a new idea. 'Men,' he exclaimed,
treating each wall to an imperious glance before continuing. 'Men, the situ . . . the situchu-chu . . . the
position is desperate . . . s'calls for stern measures.' The
Major poured himself another drink, most of which went
into the glass because he forgot to close an eye. 'Courage
is wass . . . wass we need. We need courage. And you're
all cow . . . cow . . . cows, that's wass you are, cowardly
cows. But have no fear . . . absolutely no fear. Your
leader . . . Major . . . Reginald . . . Hunter . . . Bleeding
. . . Smith has a plan. All ish not lost. We shall stand
together.' The Major got to his feet, and somewhat to his
surprise found no difficulty in remaining upright.

'Well, I did tell Miss Stopps, and that's an end to it. Oh,
darling Peter, are you very angry?' Fiona Trigg tried to
look penitent. Gregory made no reply. They were standing in the centre of the sitting-room. She put her arms
around his neck. 'Really, it's better that someone knows –
Miss Stopps agreed. She said otherwise it might be compromising for you if the Funny Farm thing is called off.'

Peter pushed the girl away from him, walked to the
window, and pulled the curtains, though whether he was
piqued or merely being practical was not clear to Fiona.

'Well, it's not likely to be called off, and it'll be a bloody sight more compromising when everybody finds out I'm half Hatch. There's going to be a hell of a bust-up here when this thing breaks officially – and I'm with Goldstein in opposition, remember?'

'Miss Stopps says it will be much better for the College if we don't get the endowment – and better for you too if nobody gets it. Then you could claim part of the money eventually.'

'So she knows that too, does she? I wish people would mind their own business.'

'Meaning me? Darling, you are my business, and I refuse to be scolded. Anyway, it was all in the *Daily Mirror*. You're not really going to refuse your Hatch inheritance if it's offered, are you?' Fiona sounded truly incredulous.

'That's just what I'm going to do.' There was no point in raising false hopes, whatever his considered intention. He looked at his watch. 'Come on, it's nearly twenty to six and we're due to scoff some of the hooch your precious Miss Stopps has provided for the JCR. I suppose it was nice of the old girl to get me invited.'

'Itchendever Hall by moonlight. C'mon, Irv, this may be the chance of a lifetime.' Amelia Hatch had put down the glass and was standing in the SCR doorway with Margaret Stopps beside her. Both ladies were dressed for an outdoor excursion; Amelia looked ready for a trip to the Arctic. She had borrowed a grey woollen scarf from Miss Stopps which was wrapped around her head and neck, covering her ears and chin. This left only her eyes, nose and mouth visible. Witaker wished it might inhibit her powers of speech. The straw hat looked even more ridiculous than usual, crammed over the wool swaddling.

'No, you go right along,' he answered as amiably as he could, 'I'll join you at firework time.' It was just 5.30. With luck he would have the room to himself when the two old birds had departed.

'The buildings are very beautiful on a fine night, Mr Witaker. Anyway, we're only taking a quick toddle around. I especially want Amelia to see the reflections in the lake.' Miss Stopps beamed at her companion; they left together, arm in arm.

Witaker was alone for the first time since the fateful meeting: alone to contemplate the undeniable fact that the impossible had happened. An apparently respectable British educational establishment was about to get its hands on this imbecile endowment, and he was powerless to stop it – powerless to ensure the half-wit who had married his daughter would inherit better than one and a half million dollars on Amelia's death. It was that same half-wit who had already invited Witaker to manage the handsome inheritance for him when the time came. This had been the slim justification for Witaker's speculating more than a little on his own account with some of the Trust funds two years ago, which in turn explained why those funds were now worth a million dollars less than they appeared to be worth on paper. Witaker needed time, or else he needed the funds of the Funny Farms Foundation distributed amongst the nine great-nieces and nephews of Cyrus Hatch, one of whom could be relied upon not to require an audit of his portion. What he did not need was a massive demand on the Trust capital to pay for extravagant enlargements to an English stately home turned university.

Irvine J. Witaker was immoral and dishonest; the fact that he had survived that way for so long indicated also that he was not entirely lacking in resource. Some time after he had begun to turn his fertile brain to assessing the several extreme courses of action open for relieving his plight, the house telephone close to where he was sitting rang insistently. He picked up the receiver. A muffled voice asked, 'Is Mr Witaker there?'

'This is he,' came the somewhat surprised reply.

'Good. Listen carefully, Mr Witaker. Unless the Funny Farms offer to endow UCI is withdrawn without delay a photographic record of your visit to a certain commercial college last evening will be issued to newspapers in this country and America by the Abu B'yat Embassy.'

Witaker tried to overcome the trembling – to make his voice sound as normal as possible – to think quickly. 'I don't know what you're talking about. Is this some kind of blackmail attempt because if it is . . .'

'Not blackmail, Mr Witaker. We're not asking you to give us money; we're telling you not to give us money. They're very good pictures by the way.'

'I shall speak to the Crown Prince without delay. He cannot be condoning . . .'

'You do that, Mr Witaker. You do that.' The line went dead.

Effect

IF THE STUDENT population of University College, Itchendever, was not much in evidence during the daytime,
there was no doubting its presence and strength after
nightfall – or so Treasure concluded after taking his leave
of Sheikh Al Haban.

Groups of young people were everywhere converging
on the south front of the Hall. There was merriment in the
air, and a good deal of raucous bantering. Torches flashed,
a few antique candle-lanterns were carried along in the
throng, providing more for atmosphere than illumination.
A well-harmonized chorus somewhere struck up 'The
First Nowell', indicating that the College choir was into
rehearsal and strong on musical timing, if ahead of
season.

Treasure had returned to his car to fetch a light top-
coat. The Rolls was parked on a wide gravelled area at the
end of the main drive on the nearside of the Hall – somewhat conspicuously parked just off the drive itself. A good
many students – presumably those 'boarded out' in the
village – passed close by. Most of them cast curious or
appraising glances at the car and its owner. One cry of
'Turn left for the Motor Show' produced a crop of other
good-humoured comments: 'Come back in an hour,
James, there's a good fellow' and 'Who's for caviare?'
preceded 'It's the Area Secretary for the National Union
of Students.'

'No,' Treasure shouted back in the general direction of
the last offering, 'I'm filling in while he's in Bermuda.'
This produced loud cheers, and passing confirmation of
UCI's much remarked distaste for student organization
outside its own tiny bailiwick.

Pink, the chauffeur, had earlier returned to London by
bus and train. Treasure had arranged to dine and spend

the night with friends in nearby West Meon – his actress wife was filming in Jamaica, and the prospect of a convivial evening followed by local golf in the morning had been more appealing than the thought of a lonely night in his Chelsea home. It concerned him only that he had expected to quit Itchendever an hour before; the further confrontation with Ribble and the Sheikh he hoped would be concluded quickly.

'Coming to get lit up?' Treasure turned from locking the car door to face a plump clergyman of middle height and age, sensibly robed in cassock and a warm black cloak that reached nearly to the ground. 'Name's Hassock – known to the undergraduates as Kneeler, well, there it is – I'm the Vicar. You a parent?' All this the Reverend Mr Hassock delivered in booming tones of great bonhomie.

'Treasure, Mark Treasure,' said the banker, shaking hands and immediately electing to enjoy the company of his breezy new acquaintance. 'No, I'm here on business – but that seems to include compulsory fireworks.'

'Ha, you don't care for fireworks. Neither do I, as a matter of fact, but it's an opportunity for a bit of social evangelizing. I'm Chaplain here as well as parish priest – strictly an honorarium job, they can't afford a full-time chap. Still, it saves me getting lumbered with an extra church.'

Treasure assumed this comment reflected more on the real difficulties of running pluralities than on Mr Hassock's professional zeal. As if to confirm this, the Vicar set an energetic pace as the two fell in together on the walk towards the Hall.

'You mean it squares the Archdeacon?' said Treasure, to advertise his understanding of such matters.

'Yes, *and* I'm the Rural Dean, so I've got it covered both ways. Ha! Come on, you miserable sinners, make way for the carriage trade.' The group of dawdling students immediately ahead parted at the loud injunction and with evident good humour. Treasure decided he had something to learn about social evangelizing.

'I've been here since before lunch and this is the first time I've seen any students to speak of.'

'Ha,' the Vicar began with the sharp expletive that peppered all his utterances, 'they spend the mornings sleeping, the afternoons fornicating, then they come out at night like hamsters – don't you, my dears?' He smiled benignly at the three or four young people who had overheard this highly libellous account; their expressions registered neither surprise nor disagreement. 'Incredible thing is, they all get good degrees. Different in my day. I got a rotten degree. Ha!'

Treasure began to feel conspicuous; perhaps a change of subject. 'Do you know the house well?'

'Born in it, my dear fellah, born in it. I'm the legendary third son pushed into Holy orders. This is my family seat – not any longer, of course. Eldest brother was killed in the war, other one's running the family business. Sold this place years ago – but we still have the gift of the living, that's how I got it. Cushy – ha!'

Mr Hassock was now pushing his way through the press of spectators assembled before the Hall, with Treasure in his wake. The crowd impeded neither the Vicar's flow of words nor his dogged progress towards an open window at the far side of the building. 'That's the JCR,' he called over his shoulder. 'They'll be serving a very fine stirrup cup through that window – courtesy of Margaret Stopps – met her, have you?' Treasure nodded pointlessly at the back of Hassock's neck. 'SCR's at the back of the building; damnfool arrangement.' The same thought had occurred to Treasure earlier. 'Anyway, we'll grab some glasses – jug as well if we can – then ascend to the holy of holies under the portico. The drink's not as good there, but the patch is reserved for VIPs – less a gathering of the great unwashed. Ha.'

The crowd in front of the trestle table set out before the window parted more in response to the Vicar's voice than to any physical effort on his part. 'Evening, Fiona,' he bellowed, 'doin' the honours, are you? Let's have one of those jugs then, there's a good girl. Where's Peter?'

Fiona Trigg was handing out glasses and jugs on the far side of the table. 'Mysteriously disappeared – in a huff,' she answered briefly, handing the Vicar a two-pint glass jug so full that part of its contents began to slop over those standing near as he carried it, shoulder high, back through the crush.

'Bless you, my children. Ha!' cried God's local steward, sprinkling stirrup cup like holy water on a Papal progress. 'Hang on to those glasses, Treasure, and steer due west up the steps. The pyrotechnics have begun.'

There was much crackling and fizzing from the lakeside as Treasure shouldered his way up the six wide steps that served the podium under the impressive portico of Itchendever Hall. The first tableau in coloured flame was in progress. The crowd cheered the momentary exhibition which was quickly replaced by the simultaneous ascent of a dozen rockets. These burst above the lake sending out an impressive shower of sparkling lights, their reflection caught upon the surface of the water.

As the display continued, Treasure contented himself with the thought that such exhibitions were usually short in duration; the cup – a concoction based on mulled claret – was really quite palatable. He stared about him but had difficulty in identifying many of those favoured with access to the special arena – clearly the privilege was not a very exclusive one since the podium was almost as crowded as the area below. The light from a battery of giant Catherine-wheels briefly lit the just-remembered countenance of the Head of Modern Languages and one or two other members of the faculty encountered at lunch. Then, on the far side of the Corinthian enclosure he spied Miss Stopps and Mrs Hatch standing at the back of the crowd and in a position that hardly afforded them a good view of the proceedings.

'I'm going to rescue some damsels in distress,' Treasure bawled into the Vicar's ear, above the noise of another shower of bursting rockets.

'Which ones? Pretty ones? Ha!' Hassock gazed about him speculatively. 'Difficult to muster a chorus-line out of this lot – that's what my wife always says, anyway.' He followed the direction of Treasure's gaze. 'Oh, you mean Margaret and what looks like a grizzly bear. They won't drink too much of our booze. Come on then.'

Hassock's intended charge through the assembled company was suspended by the first of the series of unexpected events that were destined to keep University College, Itchendever, on the front page of every national newspaper for several days – a singular achievement for so small an institution, but, sadly, one that reflected more notoriety than celebrity.

Both the Vicar and Mark Treasure were stopped in their progress by a gasp from the crowd, followed by loud cheers from the mob of students assembled, as it were, below stairs from the faculty group. The demonstration was prompted by a new, incandescent tableau at the lakeside which proclaimed in huge, triumphant red, white and blue letters the unequivocal message:

FFF

EFF

OFF

The short life-span of the medium detracted nothing from the piquancy of the message – nor was the drama of it allowed to expire with the fireworks' flame. No sooner had the more privileged spectators had time to digest the meaning and import of what had taken place than what registered as armed attack was made to supplement moral outrage. Ear-piercing bangs and blinding flashes erupted at various places on the podium causing fright and confusion amongst the academics and their familiars who, having gathered to watch a display of explosives, now found themselves featured as the main attraction.

There being no rational explanation for what was happening, irrational thought and action triumphed. Female screams, male curses and the sound of shattering glass from the columned enclosure mingled with the mounting cheers of the undergraduate horde which now began to advance up the steps of the podium on three sides. The explosions underfoot became more frequent. 'It's mined,' came one loud, deep-throated opinion, 'get back, get back.' The advice was superfluous since there was no going forwards or sideways into the solid wall of advancing studentry. 'Stand still, stand still,' came a strangled plea from another victim caught in the centre of the press, and conscious that the bombs or bullets or whatever they were seemed not be to penetrating beyond the protective periphery of the nearly captive group.

'Stop it, you young bounder,' commanded Hassock, advancing boldly down the steps, against all opposition, to grasp the arm of a student he had just observed toss a small object on to the podium.

Treasure had quickly concluded that he had become involved in a demonstration and not an intended massacre. Even so, he was concerned for the well-being of the two old ladies. A diagonal course to them being out of the question, he raced and elbowed his way along two sides of the step immediately below the stylobate. As he neared the point where he had last seen his quarries he was thankful to observe the retreating form of Amelia making resolutely for the open door of the Hall. Miss Stopps was just behind her, but then faltered and appeared to fall.

Ignoring an explosion virtually under his foot, and pushing aside a gesticulating student with the minimum concern for others in his path, Treasure reached the collapsing form of UCI's important benefactress. He planted himself behind her, pressing his left shoulder into the stalwart supporting surface of a Corinthian column. With difficulty he next grasped the lady under the arm-pits and pulled her into the shelter available on the house side of the column, out of the path of those scurrying

towards the building. Propping his charge against the
curved stone-work, Treasure knelt beside her. 'Miss
Stopps, Miss Stopps,' he cried loudly into the lady's ear,
'are you all right?'

The closed eyelids flickered, the sagging mouth
twitched at the edges, the dropped, but square, heroic
chin jerked upwards. Miss Stopps was at least alive. 'Mr
Treasure.' The eyes were now open and fully alert, the
voice strengthened, overcoming the noise of the panick-
ing throng. 'You will come to think I have a propensity
for falling off or falling over.' Miss Stopps glanced about
her. 'Are we safe here? It's my ankle; I must have twisted
it – the pain was momentarily excruciating. I think I can
stand with your help. Oh, goodness, where is Mrs Hatch?'

'Quite safe – don't worry. We'll stay here a moment.
This fool demonstration is nearly over. I think they've
run out of squibs.'

'Of what?' Miss Stopps was not dazed, just querulous.

'Thunder-flashes – bangers used by the army to simulate
the noise of battle. They're quite harmless, but thoroughly
alarming if you don't know they're coming. Anyway, all
will soon be back to normal.' This honest attempt to
reassure an upset, aged maiden lady was not nearly
justified by events. No sooner had Treasure spoken than
the hardly undisturbed night air was rent anew by the
incessant clamouring of police car sirens – their decibel
count increasing by the second in sharp contrast to the
faltering volume of student cheering. Those who had
controlled events so far were clearly not expecting such
early intervention by an almost preternaturally vigilant
constabulary.

A new kind of panic now ensued as some two hundred
joyful, victorious students simultaneously decided that
those in authority over them had reacted with wholly
uncalled-for gravity to a harmless bit of youthful exuber-
ance. Thus affronted, there was only one course open to a
student body jealous of its record for good behaviour –
and that was to run for it. The earlier reaction of the

senior members of the establishment to assault by fire-
crackers was tortoise-like when compared to the movements of their persecutors threatened by the arm of the
law.

'Oh God, I'll be sent down for certain,' moaned
Philip Clark breathlessly as he and Sarah Green raced
towards the shelter of his room in the Stable Quad.

'D'you think they're after you now?' cried Sarah, her
alarm founded on the fact that the motorized police
contingent, in three cars, instead of driving to the Hall
front was skirting the very lawn she and Peter were crossing, heading certainly in the same general direction as
themselves.

'Not the whole bloody police force.' Philip slowed to a
walk, Scottish logic replacing blind panic. 'Listen, it
could be something else that's happened – not the demo, I
mean. They've likely come from Winchester and you
can't do that in five minutes.'

As if to confirm the supposition that the arrest and in-
carceration of the JCR President was not its immediate
intention, the small army of policemen disgorging from
the cars was splitting into task groups under the direction
of a sergeant. Three, carrying loud-hailers, dashed through
the quadrangle entrance. The tail-gate of the third car –
a station wagon – was open, and two constables were
withdrawing equipment through it – metal shields,
floodlights, and what appeared to be a set of long-armed
grappling tools.

'Clear the building. Clear the building.' The sergeant
issued this echoing injunction through the microphone
and amplification unit on the leading car. Students who a
moment earlier had been scurrying towards the Stable
Quad were now being herded back on to the grass by
denizens of the law. Soon a troop of surprised-looking
residents began emerging from the quad, policemen in
their wake. Solemnly, and without haste, Sheikh Al
Haban, his son and the three members of his retinue
formed a dignified adjunct to this last group. The Sheikh

approached the sergeant at the moment when Dean
Ribble came puffing across from the direction of the Hall.

'What is the meaning of this?' Ribble addressed the
policeman as though the intrusion upon a private domain
was likely to prove as inexplicable as it would certainly
then be established as unpardonable.

'The meaning, Mr Ribble, is quite simple.' Al Haban
had stepped forward to speak. 'Some little time ago an
anonymous caller on the house telephone in my son's
room informed me that there was a bomb planted in my
motor-car timed to explode at seven o'clock. We phoned
you, and receiving no reply, we then called the police. My
men were perfectly willing to drive the car away, but we
were specifically instructed not to do so.'

'That's right, sir,' the sergeant added, 'job for experts,
this is. There's a Bomb Squad Unit on the way – should
be here in a few minutes. The bomb's not timed to go up
for half an hour – with any luck we could have it dis-
mantled by then. My blokes are doing a recce on it now.
'Scuse me.' The officer turned aside to speak with one of
his men.

'Your Highness, this is most unfortunate . . .' Ribble
began.

'Not nearly so unfortunate as what is promised, Mr
Ribble,' the Sheikh interrupted. 'Our caller warned that
next time there would be no warning.'

'Next time?'

'Oh yes, he said there would be a next time if I persisted in attempting to take over this College.'

CHAPTER X

'LILY-LIVERED LOUTS; they deserve to get locked up. Come on, Margaret, give a heave.' Hassock was assisting Treasure to get Miss Stopps on her feet. 'Keep the weight off the injured ankle. D'you think you can make it to the SCR or shall we carry you?'

'I'm all right, truly I am, Marcus. So good of you both to come to my rescue.' Miss Stopps took a tentative step forward, leaning on the Vicar's arm. 'Yes, quite all right, you see. My foot seemed to double up under me – the most temporary of strains, I do assure you. But what of Mrs Hatch? I told her to hurry into the Hall.'

'Oh, she was well ahead of the crush,' Treasure explained. Privately he wondered at the selfishness displayed by Mrs Hatch in not turning to the aid of her companion in time of need; Miss Stopps could easily have been trampled on by the retreating crowd. On further consideration, perhaps the stampede had not been as frenetic and mindless as it had seemed at the time, and Amelia might well have been swept along, unaware of Miss Stopps's accident.

'The rozzers got here in double quick time,' the Vicar observed cheerfully as the trio moved slowly towards the main doorway of Itchendever Hall. 'Ha. Interesting to see the way our revolting demonstrators upped sticks at the first sign of retribution.'

'I'm sure the whole episode was inspired by a very few undergraduates,' said Miss Stopps, defending her beloved College and its reputation. 'So foreign to the spirit that usually prevails here. No doubt the majority were simply led into what seemed a harmless prank. I blame myself in part; perhaps the stirrup cup was too strong.'

'Nothing of the sort, Margaret. Treasure and I got through nearly a pint each and we're not tipsy. Ha.

You're right in one sense though. I don't believe chucking those thunder-flashes about was part of the official programme – came as much as a surprise to most of the kiddies as it did to us. But I noted a few names and faces I've got down for excommunication. The fiery message was a bit ripe – and that was certainly expected.'

'The message, Marcus? Oh, you mean the letters – could we pause just for a moment?' Miss Stopps leant heavily on the Vicar. 'I fear I didn't understand the meaning . . .'

'And your ignorance does you credit, Miss Stopps,' put in Treasure quickly. 'Here, take my arm too – not far to go.'

'What the devil's that?' said Hassock, peering back into the darkness.

The noise of a powerful aero-engine came thrashing out of the sky from somewhere to the west of the Hall. A celestial searchlight flashed across the edge of the lake, then its restless beam raked the whole south front of the building before racing back to throw a broadening, vertical shaft of light on to a greensward of flat ground just beyond the gravelled car park. A helicopter had arrived to add to the evening's excitement, hovering like some ungainly giant bird of prey about to pounce on Treasure's Rolls-Royce – or so it seemed from where the car's owner was standing. One of the police cars, siren wailing, came racing dramatically from behind the Hall, making for the cumbersome machine as it sank to earth, its rotor blades whipping the air into frenzied gusts that raised the dust even where the trio were standing a hundred yards away.

'Ha. First time I went to a Coptic monastery in one of those things they thought I was the Second Coming. Took ages to persuade 'em I wasn't the Messiah. Couldn't blame 'em either; frightening-looking monsters – and what a racket. Here, let's get inside.'

'They must be in a hurry to get someone here,' said Treasure as they entered the almost empty hallway.

'Surely there's more to this than a student demonstration?'

'Ha. More than the little dears bargained for anyway.'

'Mr Treasure, I feel I'm going crazy. Have you seen
Mrs Hatch? – I guess I've looked everywhere except out
on the porch. Did you just come from there? Was she out
there with you?' Witaker had come pacing down the hall
towards the group. He was breathless, dishevelled, and
gave every evidence of being genuinely troubled.

'The last I saw of her she was coming in here. Have you
looked in the SCR?'

'No, it's locked. They can't find anyone with a key.'

'Well, if it was locked before the fireworks started she
can't be in there. My name's Marcus Hassock.'

'I'm so sorry,' said Treasure, remembering that the
Vicar had met neither Mrs Hatch nor Witaker. He completed the introduction. 'Have you any idea what the fuss
is all about?'

'You don't know about the bomb?' said Witaker in
amazement.

'Ha. The anarchists are here with a vengeance. What
sort of bomb?'

Miss Stopps became suddenly very agitated. 'Is anyone
in danger?'

'Is it to do with Sheikh Al Haban?' It was Treasure who
put the question that produced surprised looks from all
three of his companions, and most evidently from Witaker.

'Yes, it's in his car,' said the lawyer. 'They have police
and army personnel trying to disarm it now. I really am
very worried about Mrs Hatch.'

'I've no doubt at all she's getting her money's worth
with that crowd of sightseers outside,' said Treasure reassuringly. The hallway ran the width of the building to
the entrance on the north front, and over Witaker's
shoulder Treasure could see a throng of people on the
drive beyond. He was sure Amelia would be amongst
them, gathering a first-hand account of what was happening. 'Miss Stopps, may I leave you in the Vicar's care
while I help Mr Witaker find our straying client?'

'Of course, Mr Treasure, but do take care. Marcus, if you could stay with me. I still feel a trifle wobbly . . .'

An extraordinary meeting of the JCR Committee, hastily summoned in the Common Room itself, was sparsely attended. Due to the counter-attraction staged by police and military in the Stable Quad, Philip Clark had encountered difficulty in locating more than six members to support him in what he regarded as his hour of need. Even so, six offered some show of collective responsibility; this was a time when Sarah's lone if un-doubted loyalty failed to fill him with the same sense of well-being as her sole and uninhibited attentions in an amatory context.

'But the bomb-planting has nothing to do with us,' said Roger Dribdon firmly. 'Anyway, it's obviously not our style.'

'Yes, but that doesn't stop them thinking it's us – on top of the demo and everything. I mean, we're sitting ducks.' Philip spoke from the heart; he expected people to start shooting him at any moment.

'The demo was a properly authorized protest.'

'But it went too far. I mean, those thunder things . . . talk about ear-splitting . . .'

'And did you see Ribble's face? I thought he'd . . .'

'Order, order,' commanded Philip. 'What we have to decide is whether we take sole responsibility for the demo, or whether we . . .'

'There's no question about that.' Roger was adamant. 'If the demo achieves its object – and I think it will – we keep our part of the bargain and take the consequences. Hell, it was our idea in the first place. We asked for advice and money, and we got both – on condition we didn't talk about the source. The bomb business doesn't concern us.'

'Until they try to pin it on us. What then?' The JCR President was more conscious of the responsibility of office than ever before.

'We show them the minutes of today's meeting – that you signed.' The Secretary was intending to offer reassurance. 'They state specifically we weren't intending to protest about an Arab take-over.'

'Yet,' added the short, dark girl. 'Thank heaven Faisal's all right.' She was, as usual, ignored.

'OK,' said Philip with resignation, 'we carry on as agreed. But I still think we'll be blamed for the bomb.'

'The important thing is we stand together,' said Sarah Green as instructed. 'I mean, if they threaten to send Philip down we . . . we . . . we go down with him.'

There followed a not very noisy murmur of assent.

'Clean as a whistle. Should have been April Fool's Day not Guy Fawkes Night.' The lieutenant in the khaki flak jacket and the uniformed police sergeant gazed soberly at the monster Cadillac. The car looked even larger than life with all four doors open wide, the engine hood propped up, the boot cover standing high on its hinges, and an assortment of removable parts scattered around its hulk.

For a man who had spent a tense few minutes in the performance of a potentially very dangerous duty the lieutenant was, in the sergeant's view, singularly unperturbed. The eventual exposure of a hoax had done nothing to reduce the drama of the performance. 'I'm glad you decided not to blow it up, sir.'

'Oh, wicked waste that would have been. Wouldn't have pleased the owner either. No, there wasn't much risk once we knew there was nothing underneath. The car was locked, after all. I suppose I'd better drive it round the block. Keep the mob back till I'm clear, will you?'

The cheer that went up a few minutes later as the big black car emerged from the quadrangle entrance penetrated to the group standing around the still-locked door to the Senior Common Room.

The relief at learning the bomb scare had been a hoax

had done little to mollify the Dean. It was small consolation that someone had merely pretended to try blowing up the Crown Prince of Abu B'yat on College premises. Ribble still had to deal with the unforgiveable behaviour of the student body, as well as go through the motions of tracing Mrs Hatch. The possibility of the lady having locked herself in a lavatory had been eliminated through exhaustive search. While admitting that in the circumstances it was just conceivable she might have taken refuge in the SCR and secured the door behind her, if this were the case then she could perfectly well liberate herself by turning the key that was evidently *in situ* on the far side of the door. This much he had pointed out to the apparently distracted Witaker, while trying without success to insert his own key in the lock.

Ribble had made it plain to the growing knot of spectators around the doorway that he was a good deal more irritated about his inability to gain access to his own Senior Common Room than he was concerned about locating Mrs Hatch. It was entirely inappropriate, not to say ridiculous, that the thirty or so guests invited to sherry after the fireworks should have insult added to the injury of the demonstration as well as the frightfulness of the bomb scare by being kept waiting in the hallway. The whole situation was untenable – and, of course, as usual he was the only senior member of the staff in evidence. No doubt Goldstein had gone home to sulk. There was no sign of the Bursar whose job it was to deal with just the kind of emergency the Dean was facing single-handed. Rebellious students, disaffected Sheikhs, mislaid American matrons – he, Eric Ribble, was expected to cope unaided.

'Perhaps the kitchen door . . .' Treasure had just returned with Witaker from an outside search for Mrs Hatch.

'Is bolted from the inside,' said Ribble tersely while still attempting to dislodge the key that was blocking the entry of the one in his hand.

'What about the windows?' asked someone loudly.

'All locked apparently, someone's been to check,' Hassock volunteered. He was standing beside Miss Stopps who was occupying the only available chair in the vast, dome-topped hall.

'Impossible . . . utter . . . utter . . . quite imposshible. Doors locked . . . windows locked . . . no one inside . . . stans to reason. 'Scuse me.' Hunter-Smith elbowed his way through the crowd in an evident state of intoxication. He breathed heavily into Ribble's face; this was the last straw.

'Major Hunter-Smith . . .' Ribble began in a remonstrating tone.

'At your service, Dean.' The Bursar attempted to click his heels together, succeeded only in crossing his legs, lost his balance and was obliged to grasp Ribble by the shoulders to prevent himself falling over. 'Whoops,' he exclaimed, treating all in the vicinity to an ingratiating smile. 'Want to watch these floors, Dean. Now, if you'd let the dog shee the . . . the whatsit.' He produced his own set of keys from his pocket and attempted to select one from a dauntingly large bunch.

'I have an SCR key in my hand,' said Ribble, maintaining patience for the sake of appearances.

'S'no good in the hand. Wants to go in the lock. Want to get the door open.' Hunter-Smith attempted to steer his own key in the general direction of the keyhole.

'He's right, you know,' Treasure turned to Witaker. 'One of the windows has to be unlocked, or the thing's an impossibility. Let's go and look. Vicar, you game for a forced entry?'

'Ha – there's hardly a lock in this building I haven't raped in my time. Lead on.'

The SCR occupied the second bay to the east of the northern porch to Itchendever Hall. The room was served by five tall venetian windows of such a depth that their sills were almost flush with the paved way that separated the building from the gravel drive. Four of the windows were sash operated, but the lower half of the

centre one was a casement. 'My grandfather had that put
in to save his gouty legs,' said Hassock. 'Room was the
library in those days; heaven knows why – most of the
family were illiterate.' He shook the casement – they had
already discovered that the other windows were firmly
secured by their hasps. 'Ho, ho – the march of progress,
there's what looks like a Yale lock on the inside; used to be
a latch and bolt arrangement. No keyhole on this side,
though.'

'So people can get out but not in,' said Treasure.

'Ha, the contrivance of some houseproud female want-
ing to keep the floors clean. Got a credit card on you?'

'A what?'

'I have a Diner's Card, Mr Hassock.' Witaker produced a small plastic oblong from his bill-fold.

'They do this on television all the time – let's see if it
works.' The Vicar pushed the card through the jamb of
the doors and level with the lock on the inside. 'Like
cutting through cheese,' he said. '*Voilà*, burglars of the
world unite, you have nothing to lose but remission.' The
right half of the casement stood open before them.

Treasure entered the room, pushing aside the closed
curtains. The place was in darkness except for a glow
from the fire. 'Hang on, the light switches are by the door.'
Hassock pushed past but before he could reach his
objective the double-doors burst open. Either the Dean
or the Bursar had succeeded in dislodging the inside key
and inserting another from the outside. The room was
flooded with light; people began pouring in.

'Stop. Stay where you are – don't move, anybody.'
Treasure issued these streaming injunctions at the top of
his voice from where he was standing a few feet from the
fireplace. He had turned his back on what he had seen,
the better to shield the sight from those who were coming
in at the door.

The figure of Amelia Hatch was slumped in an armchair
to one side of the fireplace. A dagger – its handle delic-
ately traced with gold – lay on the carpet nearby. But it

was not the figure, or the chair, or the dagger that was to freeze the scene in Treasure's memory – only the blood; the blood that was everywhere. Amelia's throat had been cut from ear to ear, and she had bled copiously – bled like a pig.

CHAPTER XI

TREASURE SPOKE into the telephone in the Dean's study. 'Colin, I'm most dreadfully sorry, but obviously I can't leave. Apologize to Audrey for me, won't you? . . . The Inspector? Yes, Detective-Inspector Treet, he's with me now . . . Oh, ten minutes ago . . . Yes, extremely quick. Well, the Inspector had just arrived to tidy up the remains of a bomb scare we had earlier . . .' He took the phone from his ear and handed it to the heavily built, tousled-haired man in the crumpled check suit. 'Colin . . . er, that is, the Superintendent would like a word with you.'

'Treet here, sir.' The youthful Inspector was predictably not on Christian name terms with more senior police officers – even recently promoted ones.

But for the startling and horrifying death of Amelia Hatch, Treasure would shortly have been on his way to the West Meon home of Detective-Superintendent Colin Bantree of the Hampshire CID. The two had struck up an enduring friendship since their first meeting in the spring of the previous year. Bantree's transfer from the Thames Valley Force a few months earlier had been indirectly instigated by Treasure. The Superintendent's doctor wife had been offered a place in a group medical practice in Winchester run by a college friend of Treasure's. Bantree had applied for and obtained a Chief Inspectorship in Hampshire, and promotion had quickly followed. Treasure had welcomed the visit to Itchendever because it had given him a convenient opportunity to take up a long-standing invitation to spend a night with the Bantrees in their new home.

'Got to assume murder, sir, but it could have been suicide. Knife's on the right-hand side of the body . . . Half an hour at the most, I'd say, she's pretty warm still

... That was a hoax, sir, but it might have been a diversion; there was no bomb ... Important Arab, a Crown Prince, I think ... Mr Treasure, sir? I'll ask him.' The Inspector looked across at Treasure. 'The Superintendent would like to know if you've been alone at all during the last hour, sir . . . I mean, have you been with other people the whole time?'

'Tell the Superintendent I know exactly what he means,' said Treasure wryly. 'I've been with the Vicar of Itchendever since just before six, and we've neither of us murdered anyone since then.'

'Thank you very much, sir.' The embarrassed Treet again addressed himself to the telephone. He had some further short exchanges with Bantree before replacing the receiver. 'The Superintendent's arranging to be put in charge of the case, sir. He'll be here shortly. Now if you'll excuse me.'

The Inspector left the room – and Treasure to the thought that in police work as well as banking it was prudent to be sure one's friends were above suspicion; simply, bankers were less overt in the way they handled such matters.

'It is impossible that your friend Mr Gregory does not have a passport, my son.' Sheikh Al Haban stood calmly in the centre of his son's sitting-room. The operation he was directing required intense mental concentration from himself – and a good deal of physical effort from others.

'Father, I have looked everywhere in his rooms – it is not to be found.'

'Then look again.'

Prince Faisal shrugged his shoulders. 'Even if we find it, his condition will be questioned. The plan is complicated and dangerous. I don't mind for myself, but for you, Father, if there were a scandal . . .'

Al Haban gazed gravely at his son. 'What we are planning is the least we can do for such a service. The young man may have been misguided but it is clear he was acting in our interests. Do you suggest that we now leave him to the consequences? If he survives his attempt at self-destruction the British law will be harsh. They are keeping him on his feet next door?'

The Prince sighed in resignation. 'Yes, Father.'

'The pilot and crew are alerted, and the doctor will meet us at the airport?'

'Yes, Father. The pilot cannot guarantee clearance at such short notice but the plane is ready.'

'Then tell them to take Mr Gregory down to the car. But continue looking for the passport.'

'Father, there is another way. If I stay here – I could hide for a couple of hours – Peter could travel as me, as your son. He could wear my clothes. If you say he's ill there will be few formalities . . .'

'But what of you? You cannot disappear for ever.' But the Sheikh did not sound dismissive.

'A misunderstanding, too complicated to explain in detail. The authorities may be displeased but they can hardly do anything to me. The important thing, as you said, is to get Peter away now while there is still a chance. If you think that's what we must do I believe my plan is best.' Out of respect for his father, Faisal did not add that he thought the whole scheme was in any case a mistake.

The Sheikh pondered for a moment before replying. 'Very well. So you must, as you say, disappear immediately. Give Hassan some of your clothes – your formal robes – we can dress Mr Gregory in the car. Quickly then.'

A few moments later the semi-conscious Peter Gregory was carried from his rooms down the staircase and into the waiting Cadillac. Before the car had left the quadrangle Prince Faisal had mounted an adjacent staircase and was knocking on the door of the room occupied by the short, dark girl who served on the JCR Committee. 'Can I stay here for an hour or two?'

'Oh Faisal, you can stay all night if you want.' She experienced a nervous but altogether enjoyable tremble as the young Prince locked the door behind him.

The police constable at the main gate of Itchendever Hall had strict instructions to let no one leave. Both he and Inspector Treet, who had issued the order, were well aware that preventing egress at this and the two other road entrances to the College offered no guarantee that people would not be leaving in droves, if they wished, across the several miles of lightly-fenced perimeter. Such escape would nevertheless be difficult for motor vehicles of any size – and the Cadillac he had just waved to a halt was very sizeable indeed. He noted the absence of a front number plate, also the official pennant that fluttered above the nearside wing.

The uniformed driver lowered his window. "Is Royal 'ighness the Crarn Prince of Abu B'yat – an' if I wus you, mate, I wouldn't keep us waitin' long,' he observed cheerfully. The Cockney accent was at least reassuring; the other four occupants of the car looked, to the constable, foreign and distinctly uncommunicative.

'You can't leave – nobody can.'

'I wouldn't carnt on it – we got diplomatic immunity.' The driver leant out of the window and lowered his voice. 'I told you, 'ee's a bleedin' Crarn Prince, mate. You creatin' a international hincident or somethin'?'

Before the policeman could decide what to do next, a window was lowered at the rear of the car and a white-robed arm beckoned him. He moved the several necessary paces to draw level, then decided to salute the arm's imposing owner.

'Officer, we are now leaving. Should your superior wish to reach me he can do so through the Abu B'yat Legation. Drive on.' The constable stepped back quickly to avoid having his toes crushed as the sleek black car slid away into the night. He noted the Washington DC registration plate and started pumping the call button on his hand radio transmitter.

So it was that the curiously and hastily attired Peter

Gregory was spirited away from UCI in a state of total somnolence, and quite without his own knowledge or consent. The action was perpetrated by those convinced he had committed murder; the effect was soon to produce the same conviction in others – and all because Prince Faisal had observed his tutor leave the SCR by the casement window shortly before the fireworks began. It was the same anxious pupil who, following the bomb scare and the news of Mrs Hatch's bloody end, had rushed into Gregory's rooms to find the owner stretched out in a coma on the bedroom floor.

It was the young Prince's father who had deduced Gregory's culpability in a highly convenient homicide – too convenient for the House of Abu B'yat for there to be much doubt that it had been an act of extreme loyalty on the part of one charged with the special care and instruction of a cherished son. Gregory had been well aware of the threat Mrs Hatch offered to Al Haban's own plans for greater involvement in the College. The Sheikh had not appreciated the extent of the man's concern but the proof of it had come more as a satisfaction than as a surprise to the mind of a Middle Eastern princeling well used to hazardous expressions of regal devotion. The probability that after his selfless action this fine young man had sought sanctuary in suicide rather than in Abu B'yat had featured as the only illogical part of the affair. The possibility existed, of course, that Gregory had another and private reason for plotting his own demise and that he had seen the the elimination of Mrs Hatch as a favour to his friends which he could thus conveniently afford. In any event, the simultaneous discovery of a fairly strong pulse beat and an empty bottle of sleeping tablets had offered hope as well as elucidation. There was no way that the Arabs could have known that the bottle had been empty for several months, and that it was totally without current significance.

Al Haban was well aware that medical attention should not be delayed; equally he knew sufficient of pharma-

cology and the natural resistance of healthy bodies, even
to severe abuse, to have coolly calculated the best ordering of priorities. Since Gregory had survived so far,
artificial stimulation to his limbs would probably sustain
him on the short drive to London Airport. Once aboard
Al Haban's private jet aircraft, life – and liberty – could
almost be guaranteed. The Harley Street consultant
hurriedly summoned should be well able to cope. The
Sheikh was pleased that the discreet and competent
doctor of his choice had been so promptly available. In
fact the summons had been nearly as inconvenient as it
was certainly going to be lucrative. The doctor had made
it clear that he was on call to no one save another oil
Sheikh installed at a private London clinic for no better
reason than that he enjoyed blanket baths – a penchant
that made any requirement for real medical assistance
fairly remote. The blunt offer of 5000 dollars cash for some
airborne resuscitation and a return to London the next
day had seemed irresistible to his 'night secretary' –
neither had she taken it amiss that he had found it even
more so when she had transmitted the message to him
over the shower curtain in her Mount Street flat.

'Suicide would be much the most convenient explanation.'
Treasure shrugged his shoulders. 'Though for the life of
me I can't . . .'

  'Suicide's always the most convenient explanation for
murderers, insurance companies and lazy policemen,
Mark.' Detective-Superintendent Bantree, tall, slim, his
dark hair still as unfashionably short as it had been when
he had first met Treasure, gave his friend an understanding smile. The two were sitting in the Bursar's Office
which, together with the outer secretary's room, Bantree
had appropriated as his temporary headquarters. The
rooms were conveniently placed on the ground floor of the
Hall close to the south entrance. 'Anyway, unless the
pathologist's report throws up anything startling, suicide
is what it could be. I've known coroners come to that

verdict on flimsier proof.'

'The fingerprints on the dagger . . .'

'Are certainly the victim's. The thing was in her hand this afternoon so she could easily have pocketed it. Nobody claims to have locked or bolted those doors, and nobody was seen to leave by the only possible way out. So – ' Bantree brought his hands together as if in prayer – 'your Mrs Hatch hurried away from the student demo, locked herself in the Common Room, settled herself in front of the fire, and slit her throat, leaving us no note telling us what she did with her hat and coat. Well, no doubt they'll turn up in some cloakroom.'

'But they haven't yet.'

'No, and somehow I don't think they're going to either. Mark, the timing's altogether too tight. A lot of other people were trying to get into that room moments after Mrs Hatch came into the Hall. She just wouldn't have had time to go and powder her nose even in the cloakroom next to the Common Room *and* get there ahead of the crowd.' The policeman drummed his fingers on the desk where he was sitting. He looked up at Treasure. 'You don't think it was suicide, do you? And if you're right, somehow I don't think you're going to be giving me a golf lesson in the morning.'

Bantree had arrived at Itchendever over an hour before. In the interim he had capably supervised the activities of what Treasure considered the dauntingly large team of police and officials gathered at the College. Photographers, the police doctor, fingerprint experts, an ambulance crew – all had come, and some had gone, completing their allotted tasks with cold, impersonal efficiency. Suicide or murder: the question was of consuming, cold, professional interest. Treasure's concern went a good deal deeper. 'There's simply no reason in the world why the old girl should suddenly have decided to do herself in – and here of all places. Ask the others – well, of course, you are asking the others.'

Bantree glanced at his watch. 'Yes, but there's an

awful lot of 'em. By the time we've got statements from everybody we should have the first autopsy report – oh, and the lab test on that glass.'

'The fingerprint exercise isn't very popular.'

'Never is. The British like having their fingerprints taken as much as they like means tests – which is not at all. But somebody drank rum from that glass we found, and it wasn't Mrs Hatch. Whoever it was probably nicked the half-bottle as well – which is why no one's owned up. Silly, really; why get suspected of murder when all you've done is pocket a few tots of Lemon Hart?'

'They're sure the bottle was there?'

'Absolutely. The maid put it out with the sherry decanters ready for the influx after the fireworks. It was two-thirds full, and only to be offered to Mrs Hatch – *droit de seigneur* or *dame* perhaps. Apparently it was borrowed from the JCR before lunch.'

Treasure smiled. 'Rum is . . . was Amelia's tipple. She took our butler by surprise yesterday by demanding rum and water. I remember her joking about taking it in equal parts – with a lot of water!'

'Well, according to this American lawyer chap, what's his name?'

'Witaker.'

'Witaker. According to him she had a quick one to warm up before going out to view the Hall by moonlight – and without water because there wasn't any handy. She wasn't a lush, was she – I mean she wasn't knocking them back at every opportunity?'

'Certainly not – at least not to my knowledge. And she couldn't have been drunk this evening.'

'How d'you know?'

'Well, the admirable Miss Stopps would have noticed. She hasn't said anything, has she?'

'I don't know, I've hardly spoken to the lady. Treet is interviewing her now. No, people sometimes do themselves in during a drunken depression. That reminds me, there ought to be another dirty glass.'

'The one Mrs Hatch used? Couldn't it be the one they've found, with her fingerprints obliterated by some-one else's?'

'Tenable; even likely if the other drinker was doing it on the quiet – but the set of prints we've got here are absolutely clean, which suggests the glass was too before he or she used it. No, I think there has to be another glass – but it may not be important. That maid's not very bright so she could have cleared it away earlier and forgotten – or Mrs Hatch could have put it down in the hall, or even taken it with her. Hey, I'm glad the Foreign Office have got that Sheikh off my back – wherever he may be.'

Bantree had been irritated shortly after his arrival to learn that a whole caravan of Arabs had been allowed, as it were, to fold their tents and quietly steal away. Fortun-ately, he had conferred with Treasure before ordering the instant apprehension of the Cadillac and the detention of its passengers.

On Treasure's advice the Superintendent had person-ally telephoned the Chief Constable of Hampshire who had personally telephoned the Duty Officer at the Foreign Office, thereby goading that highly gifted and ambitious young man into welcome and creative activity. Within minutes the Abu B'yat Legation had been gratuitously informed that Her Majesty's Government had declared the person of His Royal Highness Sheikh Al Haban to be more than usually inviolate. The Security Officer at London Airport was next instructed that the Sheikh's aircraft – expectedly waiting for clearance – was to be searched for reported hidden bombs until after the time the airport closed for the night. The task completed, and the desired result underwritten, the Duty Officer at the Foreign Office only delayed returning to the letter he had been composing to his mother long enough to draft a minute about his action for the ultimate approval of the Permanent Under-Secretary – who happened to be his uncle.

'You could hardly hold a Crown Prince on a charge of

impudence,' said Treasure. 'Incidentally, I gather he took his son with him.'

'So I've been told – which means there's no one around who can tell us anything about the dagger. I suppose it did come from that wall collection.' Bantree glanced at the list of names before him. 'There's a don called Peter Gregory who they say is always in and out of Prince Faisal's rooms; he might be able to shed some light but they can't find him.'

A white light on the Bursar's internal telephone began blinking: Bantree picked up the receiver. 'Mm. All right, put him through . . . what? On the other phone, OK.' He glanced at Treasure as he exchanged receivers. 'They have twelve telephone lines into this place plus an internal system . . . Hello, yes, speaking.' He put his hand over the mouthpiece, 'It's our saw-bones.' He listened intently for some moments. 'You're sure? . . . Yes, I know, but you see the importance . . . Let me write that down.' The Superintendent scribbled two words on the pad in front of him. 'And the drug could have been lethal by itself? . . . No, I understand – stupid question . . . Fifteen to thirty minutes . . . All right, Doctor . . . I'm very glad you did . . . Of course not, that'll do in the morning . . . Oh, there's no possible doubt? Forgive me . . . No, fine, fine . . . Thank you again, and congratulations on the fast work. 'Bye.'

'Something dramatic?' The expression on Bantree's face made Treasure's question unnecessary.

'Your Mrs Hatch had a stomach cancer – reason enough to contemplate suicide if she knew about it. Trouble is, when she had her throat cut, she was probably fast asleep.'

'Asleep?'

'Drugged to the world on a massive dose of chloral hydrate. Someone laced that rum with a delayed action Mickey Finn – enough to kill a person of that age and condition, apparently.'

CHAPTER XII

THE FIRST CONSCIOUS sensation that Peter Gregory experienced was the feeling that he was floating. Then the crushing weight on his head and the difficulty he seemed to be experiencing in breathing prompted him to the quite detached and unalarmed conviction that someone was holding him under water. If this was so then he stoically charged himself to put up with the inconvenience. Some time later – he could not estimate how long – he fell to ruminating that drowning was a much slower process than he had imagined. The pressure on his head was becoming less severe. Next it seemed that his legs and arms were moving in an involuntary way: he was not commanding the movements of his limbs, but they were moving all the same. Perhaps some underwater current was exercising his extremities. The sensation was not altogether displeasing.

It was the way the driver braked the car sharply at the bottom of Egham Hill that sent Peter sliding off the seat. The two bodyguards quickly lifted him back and returned to pumping his arms and legs.

'Fools!' The exclamation registered in his mind. He tried to open his eyes; they persisted in remaining closed. Perhaps if he wrinkled his brows: his wrists and ankles seemed to be set in clamps.

'It's not easy, Highness.'

You can say that again, whoever you are: say it again – play it again – where's Fiona? Naughty Fiona; tell-tale-tit; don't be vulgar: pull yourself together; on the command – wait for it – eyes open. His eyelids parted a fraction; God, he was in a shroud – a bloody long white shroud. Perhaps he was dead already. No, he wasn't dead. Did they think he was dead? They were going to bury him. 'Fools,' he echoed weakly.

'Ah, he is coming round.' Al Haban peered over from the other side of the rear seat. 'Hold him still for a moment.' The Palestinian kneeling on the floor at Peter's feet was only too glad to rest from his awkward labour; his partner – the one who had been pumping the arms – leant back into the far corner of the seat. 'Mr Gregory, can you hear me?'

'Hearing you.' The Sheikh just caught the faint, slurred words. 'Where I am – am I – where am I?'

'You are in my car, Mr Gregory. We are taking you to London Airport. A plane and a doctor await us. You will have treatment and be in safety. Do not distress yourself.'

In your long white shroud, do not distress yourself; not much. The eyes opened wider. He found he could swivel the eyeballs; were they really bathed in treacle – in tar: see through a glass darkly; dimly. It was getting better; but he needed to play it cool – cool, man, cool. For what foul purpose was he being transported to airports and doctors? Who got him into this state anyway? Faisal's father; this was Faisal's father's car – couldn't say that quickly; think it though – *and* this was Faisal's father whispering in his ear. Up to no good; Daniel Goldstein had said it.

'Where's Faisal?'

'My son is not with us. He is in hiding until we get you out of the country. He will make a less convenient captive than you, don't you think?' The remark, which was intended to reassure, registered as distinctly sinister. So he was a captive; like hell he was. The eyeballs were moving now quite freely. He tried flexing his shoulders; the response was satisfactory. He wiggled his toes – no one could see; all clever stuff. He needed to get rid of the gorilla on his right.

'Could I have a bit more seat?' He made the voice weaker than he felt.

'Surely, Mr Gregory. Hassan, Abdul – unfold the centre seats. You can stop the manipulations.'

To hear is to obey; well, not this baby. Now where's

the door-handle? He saw a signpost as the car slowed at a
road junction: 'London Airport 1½ Miles'.

'In the matter of the American Mrs Hatch – we have
acted on the assumption . . .'

He hardly heard the rest of the words. That was it –
the rum; Mrs Hatch's flaming fire-water – that's where it
had all gone wrong. 'Bloody woman can drop dead,' he
muttered with some venom.

Al Haban caught only some of the words – but those
were enough. 'Quite – quite so, Mr Gregory. I think it
would be best if you say nothing as we pass through the
airport. I will explain that you have been taken ill. If you
would like to feign unconsciousness?'

Or alternatively no doubt we can arrange to have you
knocked on the head right now; Gregory was in fairly full
command of all his capacities, mental and physical. He
dreaded having to put them to the test but a lightning
breakaway into the arms of the first policeman in the airport building . . . 'If our Ambassador has been able to
arrange it, we may be permitted to drive directly to the
aircraft.'

Collapse of stout breakaway: the car halted behind a
small hotel baggage van waiting to join the traffic streaming out of the airport tunnel on to the big roundabout. It
was now or never. The door flew open to his touch and
weight. He paused only to slam it shut – on the fingers of
the first Palestinian; he marvelled the man did not appear
to cry out but he remembered the vacant, hurt expression.
Praise be, his legs responded to the need for instant speed.
He was clear of the Cadillac and on to the back of the
open van as it began to move away. The driver was
concentrating too hard on accelerating into the only gap
offered in the traffic to notice the impact of Peter's weight.
Cars and other vehicles closed in behind, marooning the
Cadillac at the front of the queue on the slip road. He was
safe – at least for the time being; he was also feeling un-
pleasantly dizzy.

The van on which the Australian was travelling took

the eastern exit from the roundabout, speeding up the hill beyond: nor was it obliged to stop at the next junction. Any notions its unauthorized passenger might have had of leaping off were scotched by the considerable speed at which he was being propelled, by consideration of his own condition and – decisively – by the reappearance of the Cadillac which was now closing up quickly to the rear.

The van swung round in a half-circle and stopped beneath a canopy. Peter leapt to the ground. 'Welcome to the Heathrow Hotel' said the notice; the Cadillac was stopping too. He rushed the glass doors, hitting his head because they failed to open on his thrust; then they slid aside automatically. He squeezed through a second set when the panels were barely parted. There were no police-men – only travellers; tourists – there seemed to be hundreds of them in the huge foyer. 'Help me; I'm being kidnapped.' The Japanese smiled and bowed; he had never met an Arab before. The two bodyguards were almost upon Gregory.

'Info-mation desk ova that side of loom.' The Japanese was trying to be helpful. Peter moved in the direction indicated. His head was hurting; he was feeling sick as well as dizzy.

'Mr Gregory, I think you should come with us.' The first of the bodyguards reached out towards him. He began to run towards the information desks – the empty infor-mation desks. He glanced backwards; his intended kidnappers were following at a more decorous pace. People were giving him curious glances; that was it; be conspicuous. He raced through the elevator lobby. 'Help!' A small boy with a towel was holding open one half of some wide double doors. There were steps and suddenly it was much warmer. He went down the steps, the weight on his heels. The floor was wet. There was water everywhere. The pain in his head was excruciating. 'Watch it, sir.' The waiter with the tray of drinks was immediately ahead of him. He swerved, tried to adjust the head-dress that had fallen over one eye – and slipped. He

felt his legs collapsing under him, and then he was falling.
There was a loud splash – he felt the water envelop him;
this was where he had come in.

The dark-skinned girl must have towed him to the side
of the swimming pool. She was very pretty and the badge
pinned to her bikini-top bore a legend: 'We make you feel
good all over.' The two gorillas were standing at the top
of the steps near the door. One nodded at the other; they
both turned and left. 'D'you drop in often?' asked the girl
with a giggle.

Miss Stopps swept a concentrated gaze around the small
lecture room, then fixed her eyes on those of Detective-
Inspector Treet. 'It's so difficult to fix events with the
certainty you require.' She leant forward before adding
earnestly, 'I do understand the importance, oh, believe
me I do.'

Treet was not in the least disappointed with the
testimony of the witness; the old girl was slow, but her
powers of memory and observation seemed to be in no way
impaired. He had been prepared to make allowances for
the effect of an emotional upset. There was no doubt that
Miss Stopps had been shattered by events but she was in
remarkable control of herself – much better control than
some of the people he had seen. 'If we could just recap on
a few points. You and Mrs Hatch left the SCR at exactly
five-thirty?'

'Of that I am quite sure, Inspector. It was by arrangement, as you might say. The fireworks were due to begin
at six o'clock, and I had remarked to Amelia – that is Mrs
Hatch – during tea that we should allow ourselves the
half-hour.' Miss Stopps let out a brief sigh. 'She was so
anxious to make the little tour I had suggested – to see the
Hall with the night reflections; so beautiful, you know.
I believe they would have nothing like it in America –
indeed Amelia said as much. But yes, it was half past five
when we set off – I remember referring to my watch.' She
produced the half-hunter from her bag. 'Here it is – it

keeps most excellent time.'

'And there was no one else in the room except Mr Witaker?'

Miss Stopps nodded firmly. 'That is correct, Inspector. There had been eight or nine for tea – such a jolly occasion. The others had dispersed. Mr Witaker was not inclined to join us on our walk.' She paused to ponder the propriety of her next remark. 'In truth I believe he may have welcomed the short respite – to be alone, you understand.'

Treet attempted the blunt approach. 'You mean he'd had enough of Mrs Hatch's company? Not the best of friends, were they?' Too blunt by far, and he had put a leading question.

'I should impute nothing of the kind.' The tone was quite stern. 'I meant simply that Mr Witaker might have chosen to spend some moments by himself rather than accompany two decrepit and garrulous old ladies on a sightseeing tour. Mrs Hatch and Mr Witaker appeared to me to be on excellent terms. He was very close to her late husband; a trusted family adviser.'

'About the glass of rum.' Treet changed the subject. 'The three of you didn't take a drink?'

Miss Stopps shook her head. 'Only Mrs Hatch; she noticed the cold, you know – it *is* cold for the time of year. Being used to a warmer climate, she was most careful to keep well wrapped up. The maid brought sherry and glasses after clearing away the tea – the Dean likes to entertain guests to sherry after the firework display; a traditional event, you might say. But one does not presume on hospitality.'

'You didn't take a drink?' Miss Stopps nodded. 'And the half-bottle of rum was brought in with the sherry for Mrs Hatch?'

'Not necessarily for Mrs Hatch at that moment but for her eventual consumption, yes. But since we were going out . . .'

'And since it was cold, she took a nip there and then.'

'That is correct, Inspector.' Miss Stopps did not volunteer her views on the degree of presumption permitted to rum drinkers as opposed to those who consumed sherry. Treet thought it unnecessary to ask. 'Neat,' she added.

'Sorry?'

'She drank it neat. There was no water available. I offered to obtain some but she would not hear of it.'

'Mr Witaker didn't volunteer to get the water?'

'He was some little distance away . . .'

'Sitting on the other side of the room. And so far as you remember she replaced the empty glass on the table?'

'I assume that to be the case, Inspector. As I explained, I left to get my coat and when I returned Mrs Hatch was standing near the table.'

'But she didn't have the glass with her when she left the room?'

Miss Stopps appeared confused. 'Why should she have taken the glass with her? Oh, I see. No, I don't believe so.'

'Nor the bottle?'

'Certainly not the bottle.'

Treet nodded to the detective who had been taking notes at the end of the short table where they were all sitting; the man closed his book and left the room. 'And nothing Mrs Hatch said or did while she was with you suggested abnormal depression – or the sense that she was under any kind of threat?'

'Nothing at all. We spent a most enjoyable half-hour. She was so absorbed and appreciative we were very nearly late for the fireworks.' Miss Stopps paused. 'Had we been earlier . . . nearer the front of the gathering, surely she would not have been first to reach the Common Room? I do so blame myself – and my stupid fall . . .'

Treet was not a particularly compassionate man but he was moved to a display of genuine sympathy by these sorry admissions. He stood up, and taking Miss Stopps's arm, helped her out of her chair. 'I'm sure you've nothing to reproach yourself with, ma'am. If Mrs Hatch was going to do herself . . . to do away with her life, she'd have found occasion, no doubt.'

'You think it was suicide, Inspector?'

'Too early to say yet.' But only just; Superintendent Bantree was standing in the doorway. 'Would you like someone to see you home, Miss Stopps?'

'Thank you, no. Most kind, but I have my car.' Treet and Bantree stood aside to allow Miss Stopps to leave. She gave them both an approving nod before setting off down the corridor to the hallway, her limp perceptibly improved.

'That's the last of the principals, sir,' said Treet, consulting the list of names in his hand. 'Except for Mr Gregory, and we still have some students to see, but . . .'

'Never mind that for the moment, Alan; things are on the move.' Bantree related the information he had received following the police autopsy.

'So it's murder, sir.'

'Well, people don't cut their throats when they're laid out by strong sedatives. She'd taken – or been given – ten times the normal dose of the stuff, fifteen to twenty minutes before her throat was cut. Doctor says she must have been semi-conscious at the very best – more probably out like a light.'

'Was it tablets, sir, or what?'

'Liquid – it comes in 500 mg. capsules. She'd had the contents of at least ten – in alcohol; rum. It couldn't have tasted very nice but rum's pretty pungent, and if she knocked it back fast . . .'

'So we're assuming it was involuntary, sir.'

'She drank it; that's all we know for sure. We shan't have the full autopsy report until the morning; so far the timings sound wrong. She comes in from the fireworks in a panic at six-thirteen or fourteen, and locks the Common Room door behind her . . .'

'Because the students have scared her stiff.'

Bantree nodded. 'She takes a quick snort to calm her

nerves; maybe she adds the sedative herself but gets the dosage wrong. Fifteen minutes later her throat's cut and she dies almost immediately. Mr Treasure and the others broke into the room at six forty-four.'

The Inspector glanced at his note-book. 'I was there at six forty-eight, sir. The body was very warm; the timing . . .'

'The body was parked in front of a large fire. The timing or the doctor's wrong. According to him, Mrs Hatch died about six o'clock.'

CHAPTER XIII

'But, Colin, you haven't met the chap – I have. I tell you he's no more capable of murder than you are.'

'The most improbable people find criminal capacities – given the right motive.'

Treasure and Bantree were once more closeted in the Bursar's Office. The remains of some ham sandwiches with three coffee cups lay on the desk between them. Inspector Treet had left a moment before – and promptly on the telephoned news that the doctor who looked after the medical needs of the College had returned home.

'Promotion's made you pompous.'

'But not half-witted. Gregory had the motive; he found himself with the opportunity, so he took it. Impulsive sort of chap, is he?'

Treasure shook his head. 'Don't know him well enough. But what you suggest is pure speculation.'

'Partly, I agree, but it has a factual base. According to his girl-friend, his mother was a Hatch – incidentally, d'you really know her father?'

'Mm, we were at school together; he's a stockbroker – older than me.'

'Well, let's not allow the system to cloud our judgement.' In return for this jibe Treasure made a gesture indicating what he thought of inverted snobbery; Bantree's background – unlike his own – had been short on privilege. 'Witaker says if Gregory is the right kind of Hatch he comes into one and a half million dollars now the old girl's dead.'

'So does Witaker's daughter, and eight other people.'

'But they're not all here. Not that I didn't fancy Mr Witaker in the role of crooked family lawyer. We'll keep him in fall-back position – but he's a long way behind our golden boy from Australia.' Bantree checked a note on some papers under his coffee cup. 'Gregory – seen at five forty-five or thereabouts storming out of the JCR after a slight tiff with the lovely Fiona. Next sighted at eight-ten when he was fished out of a swimming pool at London Airport lightly disguised as a wet Arab. Now detained for questioning at West Drayton Police Station until I decide what to do with him.' Treasure tried to interrupt. 'I haven't finished; you wanted the facts. Prints taken from various parts of Gregory's rooms match those on the used glass found at the scene of the crime, now known to have contained rum and knock-out drops. OK – now for deduction, or if you prefer, supposition. Gregory is not seen by anyone either at the fireworks or in the crowd watching the bomb scare diversion – so he gets zero for interest and curiosity if he didn't have something pretty important to do.'

'Would you watch fireworks if you weren't made to?'

'Maybe not, but if I was on the staff here – hell, even if I wasn't – I'd find a bomb disposal unit, plus a ruddy helicopter, fairly compulsive viewing.'

'Perhaps he was in the crowd and nobody saw him.'

'Or perhaps he was in the SCR – correction; we know he was in the SCR at some point, ready to comfort Mrs Hatch with rum. Possibly he pours the stuff down between her quivering lips, waits a decent interval, and slits her gizzard. He then, as they say, makes good his escape in cahoots with a Middle Eastern prince – God knows why, and the prince ain't telling.'

'No jury would . . .'

'We're a long way from a jury, Mark, but if Gregory's innocent he's behaving in a very strange way.'

'The same applies if he's guilty. He's not stupid, you know. Why should he have gone out of his way to call attention to himself like this if . . .'

'Panic, remorse – you seem to think he's a decent chap at heart.' Bantree finished with a smirk.

'Nonsense – I mean, your whole scenario's absurd. Are you seriously suggesting Gregory organized the student demonstration and the bomb scare on the long chance of getting Mrs Hatch to himself in the SCR so he could do her in?'

'Somebody organized 'em . . .'

'But with the certainty of getting Mrs Hatch into that room – alone?'

'With the certainty that all but the geriatrics would be fighting for ringside seats elsewhere.'

'So he managed to trip up Miss Stopps as well?'

'Miss Stopps's fall may have saved her life.'

'You mean he'd have done for them both? Well, Miss Stopps doesn't drink rum.'

'How d'you know?'

'I don't, but she was drinking sherry before lunch.'

'If you were an old lady scared out of your wits, what would you take – rum or sherry?'

'Tea.'

'Don't be obtuse – one of your favourite expressions. The whole point of having the chloral hydrate handy was so he could cope with more than one victim at leisure – knock 'em out, then cut 'em up . . .'

'Relying on the necessary fifteen uninterrupted minutes for the drug to take.'

'Hence the second diversion – the bomb scare.'

'Colin, it's all too elaborate and . . . and risky. I mean, what if the Vicar and I had gone round to that window a few minutes earlier; we'd have met the chap coming out.'

'Pity you didn't. As it was, you couldn't have missed him by much.'

'Unless the killing was earlier than we think – and incidentally it has to be a hell of a lot later than your police surgeon says.'

'Doctors are far from infallible – remember I married one.'

'Audrey's a highly qualified paediatrician.'

'They're the worst.' Bantree snorted. 'She was certain I had an ulcer last summer – had me X-rayed, barium mealed, sucking pills the size of dinner plates. D'you know what it was? Constipation. God, what I owe to All-Bran.'

'So you're not buying the police surgeon's timing?'

'Well, obviously I'm not buying six o'clock or earlier as the time of death. It'll be later than that when we get his report tomorrow – you'll see. He knows already the corpse was watching fireworks at six-ten observed by you, the Vicar, Miss Stopps and heaven knows how many others before it beat a miraculous retreat into the Hall, also impressively witnessed. Pity I told him that when I rang him again; got him back-pedalling like mad – started mumbling about over-compensating for the effects of fire on body heat. Anyone'd think we're investigating arson. Come in.'

A uniformed policeman entered holding three closely-typed sheets of headed paper. Bantree looked pleased. 'Intelligence from West Drayton, no doubt.' He glanced at the top sheet. 'Yup, this is Gregory's statement . . . ho, ho, plus a line or two volunteered by your friend the Sheikh via the Abu B'yat Legation via the Foreign Office. Protocol has been observed. What is it, Jones?' He looked up at the policeman who was still standing beside the desk.

'Young gentleman waiting to see you, sir, one of the students, name of . . .'

'Put him on to one of the sergeants.'

The policeman persisted, 'Name of Prince Faisal, sir. Says it's important, sir.'

Bantree glanced at Treasure. 'Ask him if he'd mind waiting a moment, will you? Outside, is he?' The officer nodded and withdrew. 'So; the missing heir.'

'D'you want me to clear out?' asked Treasure, making to rise.

'No, you know him, and that might help. Besides, you can stop me putting my foot in it – like you did earlier. We'll make it informal; I can always get a proper statement later. But let's see what Gregory has to offer first.'

The Superintendent began scanning the report. 'Mm . . . left the JCR at five-forty-five – that checks – heading back to his rooms . . . went into the SCR to pick up a book . . . place was empty . . . helped himself to a drink . . . neat rum . . . put used glass on table by the window . . . left by the casement door which was latched back – ' Bantree looked up – 'he assumed on the order of higher authority so he left it that way . . . reached his rooms, he thinks, at five-fifty . . . felt drowsy, and the next thing he knows, he's in the Sheikh's car approaching London Airport . . . believed at the time he was being kidnapped . . . now thinks differently – very convenient – shocked to hear about Mrs Hatch . . . et cetera, et cetera. Medical test shows high content of unspecified sedative in his bloodstream.'

'So he dosed himself with chloral hydrate to get over the shock of murdering Mrs Hatch,' remarked Treasure impassively. 'What's the Sheikh say?'

Bantree turned to the last sheet. 'His son found Gregory unconscious in his bedroom at about six-fifty-five – after the bomb scare business was over . . .'

'And after the news was out about Mrs Hatch,' Treasure interrupted.

'Right. Oh, here's the juicy bit. His Highness decided to get Gregory to a doctor – and since he had a Harley Street man waiting at London Airport he drove him straight there . . . doesn't know why Gregory broke away but appreciated he was in a highly nervous state.'

'That's not nearly so incredible as you may think, Colin. Rich Arabs fly two thousand miles and more to see Harley Street doctors. A fast drive to Heathrow for the same purpose would have seemed perfectly logical to a chap like Al Haban.'

The Superintendent appeared unconvinced. 'And you suppose he has expensive medical attendants permanently hanging about at Heathrow on the off-chance . . .'

'Oh, of course he sent for the chap, but so what?'

'So there's more to it. And why did he dress Gregory

up like a Bedouin?'

'Why not ask his son?'

'Good idea.' Bantree stood up and walked to the door.
'Prince Faisal – how d'you do, sir. Come in, won't you? I
believe you know Mr Treasure.'

Witaker lay fully clothed on the bed in the UCI guest
suite. It was not a particularly luxurious apartment, but it
did have its own bathroom so that no one had seen or
heard him being sick. The reaction had been predictable –
it had been that way since he was a boy. How he had
staved it off for three hours – what was it now, yes, nine
o'clock – he would never know. He told himself to be
calm; it was all over. Pray God he would never have to go
through such an experience again. God our very help in
trouble. God helps those who help themselves. God
protect me. Yes, settle for protection; forgiveness was for
those who couldn't justify their actions. He, Irvine J.
Witaker was justified. He was also in the clear; that was a
comforting thought. Hang on to that – relax or you'll be
sick again: forget Cyrus.

The police interview had been the worst bit; but his
urbanity had seen him through. Ribble, the Dean, had
been a good deal less obsequious now his million dollars a
year endowment had evaporated. Bad luck, Mr Ribble;
it's an ill wind that blows nobody any good, though.
Cyrus used to say that. Get Cyrus out of your head. Stay
the night, Ribble had said – pyjamas and shaving gear
would be provided. Other arrangements could be made
in the morning; thank you for nothing because you are
getting nothing. Use the telephone in my room; you will
need to telephone America. No mention of charges; you
could see it in the man's eyes, though – mean, count-the-
cost, money-grubbing eyes; like Cyrus.

They had been shocked in Pittsburgh; *they* had been
shocked. Precisely what time did you leave the Common
Room? To be precise – drop dead, you peasant policeman,
because you are pinning nothing on me, because there is

nothing you can pin on me. You may keep your severed heads – your unspeakable obscene photographs. No bargains now; no need for bargains; no money for this down-at-heel apology for a university. Feed it to the Arabs with the sheep's head – sheep's eyes. You are safe; stop shaking. It's all in the mind; the haunting is in the mind. The eyes, that ghastly head. Cyrus is dead.

'Nice chap.'

'You handled him very well.'

'You mean I haven't upset international relations.'

Treasure smiled at his friend. For someone who affected not to be impressed by inherited rank Bantree had been perceptibly deferential to the young prince. If the attitude had been a calculated one it had certainly paid a dividend. 'Does the bit about his father intending to smuggle out Gregory as Prince Faisal have to go in the record?'

'Not if you think it'll stop our oil supplies.'

'It's not that; Faisal will be in terrible trouble with his father for losing him face. After all, they didn't even reach the airport.'

'Felonious intent – *and* they thought they were helping a murderer to escape: he didn't admit that, but it's pretty obvious.' The Superintendent quickly held up his arms in a gesture of surrender in response to Treasure's look of exasperation. 'All right, I'll go quietly. It wasn't my fault, me lud,' he mimicked, 'it was a rich bankin' interest wot made me suppress the evidence.'

'Thank you, Colin,' said Treasure seriously, and not entirely unconscious that he had just done a service for a prospective client. 'It was a fair swop, you know,' he added in self-mitigation. 'The boy was pretty forthright – I would judge totally honest in what he told us; granted he left a bit unsaid – but he still told us a lot.'

Bantree nodded. 'Agreed. If Al Haban thought Gregory had bumped off Mrs Hatch it's pretty certain he hadn't arranged for one of his own people to do it.'

'They're all accounted for anyway, you know. They were all there when I left the Sheikh at five-forty.'

'Except the chauffeur.'

'Who you said was having high tea with the porter and his wife before the two of them were sent for over the bomb scare.'

'Right. You left when the French tutor arrived . . .'

'He came five minutes before he was due, that's why I noted the time. Dithering old chap.'

'Yes, he only does private tutoring, ex-schoolmaster who lives locally. He's all there, though. He witnessed Al Haban take the phone call about the bomb just after six. Up to then the Sheikh and the two bodyguards never left the room. Prince Faisal tactfully withdrew to the bedroom for five minutes while the old guy was making his report . . .'

'Which is how Faisal came to see Peter Gregory leaving the SCR.'

'Well, he says he did . . . at ten to six. I want that re-enacted. It was dark, there were a lot of people about.'

'Yes, but Faisal admitted he only thought it was Gregory at first and wasn't sure until he'd crossed the lawn and walked under a light near his window.'

'After the anonymous phone call Prince Faisal went to get Gregory but figured he'd gone out again . . .'

'He only looked into the sitting-room and called out. The police must have done the same when they were evacuating the building later.'

'And all the time Gregory was flaked out on the bedroom floor. It fits together all right. The whole group was under the eye of the police from about six-twenty.'

'Which gets them and Gregory off the hook whatever time the murder was done.'

'I'm not moving that fast,' said the Superintendent cautiously, 'but I admit it looks that way. Lucky Al Haban detests fireworks, otherwise they'd just be part of the communal alibi. When did the Prince say he missed the dagger? – four o'clock, was it?'

'Yes – when he and his father got back from their constitutional. Why d'you suppose the murderer risked pinching it?'

'Well, it's sharp for one thing – and it's wasted a good deal of our time for another. As far as I can see, half the College were in that room some time today, and I dare say the other half could have been if they'd wanted, and no one the wiser.'

'Certainly I don't think the Dean had any right to take us in there. I told you I felt like a trespasser.'

'Mm, that was a pity – if you'd stayed you might have noticed if the thing was still there when you all left.' Bantree hesitated. 'The Dean said Mrs Hatch was the only one actually to handle it. The Bursar chap's not sure or he was too drunk to remember. Shame we've exploded the suicide idea – it fitted that nicely.'

'But the murderer must have known you'd . . .'

'Get on to the drugging? Probably, but not necessarily. People have blank spots. Anyway, we don't know for sure the murderer knew about the doped rum.'

Treasure looked surprised. 'You mean there could have been two people doing down Mrs Hatch unknown to each other?'

'Two or more – some a great deal more earnest than others. You must have figured that for yourself, Mark. There are at least half a dozen people who in your own hearing spoke out against the Funny Farms project . . .'

'But they're not all murderers.'

'They don't have to be to make my job more difficult. And there are some who haven't shown their hands. What about the awful warnings – the sheep's head and the other uncooked offerings?'

'Student protests like the fireworks.'

'Well, you can cross off the fireworks for a start. Those kids were put up to doing what they did.'

'You know that?'

'No, not for certain, but I can smell a true testimony from a cover-up a mile off. There's altogether too much owning up in the student statements. Everybody's taking the blame for everything. And don't forget the anti-Arab bit. Was the bomb hoax part of the murder plan or a completely independent firm? The only common thread is a determination to keep this College the way it is. We could be dealing with a lot of little people or one cunning, pathological intellect – ' Bantree sighed – 'or both. And there's no shortage of brilliant intellects amongst this lot. What have you got, Alan? Hot outside, is it?'

Inspector Treet had entered the room looking like an overweight long-distance runner facing the last lap. He flopped into a convenient chair making some attempt to mend his untidy appearance. 'Flat tyre in the village.'

'Should have left the driver to change it.'

'I did.'

Bantree chuckled. 'Well, you could have fooled us. Come on, what'd you get from the doctor? Co-operative, was he?'

'Not unco-operative – just unsystematic. No file cards, no records of any sort so far as I could see; ought to be a law.' He was recovering his breath. 'Anyway, he doesn't give strong sedatives to students on principle; fobs 'em off with low-strength tranquillizers in small quantities – very small. Doesn't mean they don't get stronger things in the holidays, of course.' He treated Bantree and Treasure to a meaningful look; Treet and the doctor evidently shared a considered suspicion about the depths of student depravity and duplicity.

'What about the staff?' asked Bantree.

'Different story entirely; dishes out drugs like Smarties. Far as I can see people practically write their own prescriptions. There's someone – he wouldn't say who – hooked on cough mixture containing morphine. Can't sleep without it. But there are only two other serious insomniacs – they get chloral hydrate. Here's the proprietary name.' Treet produced a crumpled piece of notepaper from his pocket and handed it to Bantree. 'He didn't want to tell me the names of the patients at first –

or he'd forgotten them. Anyway I came the heavy policeman and he eventually coughed up. One isn't technically a member of the staff – I asked him first only for the names of staff members on the stuff.'

'Well, who are they?' Bantree was showing uncharacteristic impatience.

'Mr Ribble – that's the Dean – and Mrs Daniel Goldstein.'

CHAPTER XIV

TREASURE GLANCED at his watch; it was nine-fifteen. He walked across the hall to examine the plan of the College interior exhibited near the main entrance – this in preference to asking someone the way to the guest suite. The internal arrangements of old houses interested him as much as their exteriors; outsides were for looking – insides for living. Grandiose romantic or classical façades usually involved hideous inconvenience for the high as well as the lowly who had elected or been chosen to dwell behind them. In a great house such as Itchendever fallen to institutional use he enjoyed deducing unaided the former designation of rooms put to purposes that the original owners would have found bizarre or incomprehensible. Here was one – on the first floor – 'Careers and Moral Guidance', a combination which, after the words of Noel Coward, might have been calculated specifically to damp the fun of some former eldest son: a guest bedroom no doubt, but not for a guest of consequence, placed as it was at the maximum distance from stair-head and the nearest water-closet.

The plan was more difficult to decipher historically than most of those Treasure had come across. The ground floor in particular seemed to have more small rooms than he had expected. Doubtless there had been latter-day subdivisions; perhaps he would cheat and go over the thing with the Vicar. It was then, quite inconsequentially, that he remembered why the name Hassock had been familiar to him: he must ask about that too. Meantime, the room he was looking for . . .

'Mr Treasure – has Faisal made it all right for Peter?'

'Hello, Fiona.' The girl was evidently agitated. 'Yes, I think so.' She was pretty; strange, when young, her father had borne a distinct physical resemblance to an elderly

elk; nowadays he looked like a middle-aged elk; attractive
wife probably – Treasure had never met the lady. 'I gather
you smoked him out. Good thing you did.'

'He was hiding on purpose – it wasn't difficult to guess
where.' Treasure considered that a knowledge of Itchendever mating habits was probably the first essential of
College communications. 'Are they bringing Peter back?
– he hasn't done anything; honestly.'

'He's getting a free ride home, I believe.' Treasure said
this lightly and to avert any suggestion of prison vans and
manacles. 'The Superintendent has some questions to put
to him – but I wouldn't worry.'

'He was just upset because . . . well, because I let on to
Miss Stopps about his mother. I put my foot in it, didn't I,
telling the policeman . . . you see, I thought they knew –
that they were after Peter because of the money he'll get.
But he's not going to take it – that's the whole point. Oh
God, I am a twit.'

'No, you're not. It would have come out in the end
anyway – better to get it all cleared up. Peter's accounted
for at the critical times – assuming the medical evidence
proves he swallowed enough of that dope to have been
unconscious from about six o'clock – and I think it does.
So cheer up.' He smiled. 'Are you very fond of him?'

'We're going to be married.'

'Father approve?'

'He will when I tell him; he's a darling.' The lovable,
middle-aged elk.

Treasure had an idea; Witaker could wait for a bit.
'D'you know the JCR President? – Clark, isn't it?'

'Yes. Philip.'

'Could we find him? – I'd like a word.'

'He's in his room with the others – I just left them.
They're having a council of war. Come on, I'll show you.'

Philip Clark's room was two staircases along from
Prince Faisal's in the Stable Quad. They passed a uniformed constable on the way, vigilantly drinking coffee
under the arch to the quadrangle, while metaphorically

closing the stable door.

Brief introductions were completed by Fiona to the four occupants of the room. There followed an embarrassing silence while Treasure considered how best to bridge the generation gap after accepting the only comfortable chair, vacated in deference to his seniority. He carefully examined the Lamb's Navy Rum poster. 'Listen,' he said, 'I'm not a policeman.'

'He's a banker,' offered Fiona from the bed where she had positioned herself next to Roger Dribdon. Sarah Green and the short, dark girl (the latter's Arabian night disappointingly foreshortened) were seated on the floor.

Treasure addressed himself to Philip who was sitting across from him in a creaking, wickerwork armchair. 'I do have a semi-official connection with the College and . . . you may find this difficult to believe but I don't entirely disapprove of the demo tonight.' The atmosphere perceptibly lightened. There was an encouraging creak as the JCR President slackened his upright position. Only the short dark girl found it difficult to concentrate; she was wondering about Faisal's future intentions – assuming he had any – and whether she should start taking the Pill; the supply she had was more than a year old – they might have gone off. 'I probably shouldn't be telling you this but the police don't believe you've entirely come clean with them.' Shades of Humphrey Bogart; try again. 'They think you may be holding something back – probably with the best of intentions. Now they're pretty thorough, you know, and this *is* a murder investigation, so they'll probably get to the truth in the end.'

Treasure paused and looked around at the faces. Roger Dribdon wore a wooden expression, but Sarah and Philip exchanged glances that at least registered comprehension. 'What they think,' he continued, 'is that the demo was perhaps not entirely your own inspiration – that someone else was involved – not a student. If that's so, then it could be as much in that person's interests as your own for the truth to come out now.'

'Why?' asked Roger.

'Well, let's assume the demo had nothing to do with the murder.'

'It didn't.' Again this was the JCR Secretary.

'Fine; but the police can't be sure of that until they have all the facts – until they do, the demo will be a loose end and they're not going to leave it dangling.'

There was another pregnant pause broken appropriately by the short, dark girl. 'Philip, I think we should . . .'

'Shut up, Dolores,' Roger cut in. 'If we told you there was someone – and I'm not saying there was – but if that someone hadn't known what form the demo would take, wouldn't even have approved, just sort of suggested there should be some kind of protest during the fireworks about the Funny Farms business, and put up the cost. I mean someone who couldn't possibly have had anything to do with the murder . . .'

'All the more reason you should tell the police – or me.'

'And you'd use your discretion about whether to pass it on or not?'

The banker nodded. Philip Clark, as though suddenly conscious of his status as putative head of the student body, leant forward earnestly to the accompaniment of loud creaks. 'I think we should tell you. It was . . .' He looked around at the others. 'It was Miss Stopps.'

Treasure burst out laughing.

'Come in.' Witaker willed himself to look composed. 'Oh, Mr Treasure, I'm glad to see you. I thought it might be the Dean.'

'I've just dropped in to see how you're coping – to see if there was anything more I could do. Did you get through to the States all right?'

'Surely. I've alerted all the necessary people. A terrible shock to everyone, of course. I fear the media . . .'

'Will have a field day.' Treasure nodded. 'I have our own public relations people standing by. The police are being very helpful. Superintendent Bantree held up the official announcement as long as he could, but with so many people in the know . . .' He shrugged his shoulders. 'The Bursar is sobering up by the minute; he should be capable of handling awkward callers later tonight.'

'Wretched man. If it hadn't been for him we'd never have . . .'

'I know exactly how you feel. Anyway, this place is private property and the police have instructions not to let reporters and cameramen through the gates – not that any have shown up yet. You shouldn't be harassed to-night.' He glanced at the house telephone on the bedside table. 'That's not an outside line. The police are manning the switchboard so all calls are being routed through them. Now, you look as though you could use a drink.' Treasure's unspoken view was that the man could use a week in a rest home; he looked desperately worn and haggard.

Witaker had been warned not to mix tranquillizers with alcohol – but the relative sense of well-being the drug had already produced served to weaken his resistance. 'There's nothing I'd like more.'

'Come on then; I can't leave Itchendever until Bantree does and I should think that means an hour at least. There are several pubs in the village. Let's pile into my car and honour one of them with a visit; do us both good to get away from this place for a bit.'

Witaker was glad enough to fall in with this plan – as glad as the Superintendent had said he would be.

The big bosom heaved in exasperation. Mrs Hunter-Smith removed her gaze from the shame-faced figure of her husband and sought solace in the Peter Scott reproduction framed over the fireplace. 'So,' she said deliberately, addressing the leading duck, top left of the picture, 'you explained to this Inspector that while you probably didn't do the murder, you can't be sure because you were drunk at the time.'

'Nothing of the sort, my love – you're twisting my words.' A man could surely expect sympathy and understanding from his own wife at a time like this.

'You told him you were drunk?'

'He knew I was a bit cut when he interviewed me, and anyway the others had said . . .'

'Others – what others?' She examined the rest of the ducks accusingly.

'Well, the Dean for one – he was angry about the locked door.' Why should he be standing here like a corporal on report? He had slaved and plotted for this half-colonel's daughter – a half-colonel who had incidentally never made colonel, and ended up dependent on *him*. 'I said I'd been busy in my office from after tea, had one or two, and then went to look for Mrs Hatch.'

'Who was found with her throat cut soon after.' The eyes now closed, but not in sleep. Daddy had said the man was a fool – after they were married. 'Why did you say you were looking for Mrs Hatch? There were at least three hundred other people you could have been looking for and none of them was murdered.'

'Because it was the truth – honesty's the best policy.'

'You mean you were too drunk to think up a convincing lie. And you saw no one at all – except for . . .'

'Not that I can remember,' he interrupted. 'I looked in the SCR but it was empty, then I went up to the Dean's room and he wasn't there . . .'

'And that's when you left the letter saying you were fed up with UCI and leaving for Torchester?' Her mother had said she could do better if she waited; twenty-eight had been no age for a girl with her attributes. Mrs Hunter-Smith steeled herself again to regard the man she had married: he flinched under the withering glare.

'It was what we'd agreed. You said I should stop Mrs Hatch . . .'

'I didn't say you should cut her throat.'

'I didn't cut her throat.'

'No, but the police obviously think you did.'

'I meant to tell her I'd lost confidence in UCI and she'd be better putting her money into Torchester. Dammit, it was I who brought her to Itchendever in the first place; she seemed to like me – she might have taken my advice.'

'And if she hadn't taken your advice, you might have got fighting drunk . . .' Mrs Hunter-Smith had no real doubts about her husband's innocence; for one thing, she harboured the unjustified belief that he lacked guts. What troubled her was that he had probably spoiled the next move in what could only charitably be described as his career pattern – this time before even he had made it. And to think that if she had stayed single and in the Army . . .

Why did he have to suffer a hangover and humour a harridan? 'Look, the police can't really suspect me. I had no motive to kill Mrs Hatch. Now she's dead the money won't go to UCI or Torchester.'

'*I* didn't know that – why should they think you did?'

'I've told you – it was common knowledge.'

Mrs Hunter-Smith ignored all common things. 'And if Torchester had cancelled your job because the money was coming here – I suppose that wouldn't have given you a motive?' The same thought had occurred to Inspector Treet.

'Of a sort, yes, but . . .'

'But you were too drunk to think it through.' She glared at the ten-year-old, black-and-white television receiver; she had set her heart on seeing the Royal Tournament in colour next year.

'Look, I've got to go back. I only came over to shave and change. I'm supposed to deal with reporters and people – God knows when I'll be finished.'

'Well, make sure you tell that policeman about who you saw skulking in the dark on the SCR terrace.'

'He wasn't exactly skulking.'

'Well, that's what it sounds like to me. What business did he have there anyway? I've always thought he wasn't to be trusted; none of that sort are.' Mrs Hunter-Smith's prejudices, like her social ambitions, had withstood the test of time.

'That's not very charitable, my love.'

'Neither is murder.' Specified genocide or euthanasia in a good cause and on a big enough scale would not have prompted such heavy condemnation.

He climbed the stairs feeling as though a lead weight was pressing on his head. He would have given anything to be going to bed. While he waited for the Alka-Seltzer to dissolve in the glass on his dressing-table he was consoled by a flicker of pride as he regarded the five medals framed in their case on the wall. One had a clasp; it witnessed that he had been mentioned in dispatches for an act of bravery. While leading a reconnaissance patrol before the Battle of the Bulge he had stabbed to death two German sentries – because shooting them would have been too noisy. He had been drunk that night too.

CHAPTER XV

Treasure had chosen The Rod and Fly because it proudly proclaimed its status as a 'Free House' on an appendage to the inn sign outside. As a child he had always imagined that such designation indicated that drinks were dispensed gratuitously to all comers. Age had brought enlightenment along with disenchantment in this as in so many other contexts. Nevertheless, given choice and opportunity, he preferred to apply his limited bar custom to that diminishing group of pubs that did not owe allegiance to any particular brewer. This at once gave him the feeling that he was supporting private enterprise in one of its most basic forms as well as securing the widest choice of branded intoxicants. Since he invariably drank either Carlsberg Lager or Ballantine's Whisky – depending on the time of day – the benefit of selection was largely an academic consideration. Since no one had yet succeeded in nationalizing licensed premises it was questionable also whether the powerful brewers did not provide a better defence against state encroachment than a handful of freehold publicans.

The saloon bar of The Rod and Fly was, as usual, practically empty for reasons quite unconnected with brand range or ideology. Draught beer served within its close-carpeted precincts was a penny a pint more than it was in any other part of the same premises or in any other bar in the village.

The banker and the American lawyer sat on padded stools at the end of the bar counter. Treasure was on his second lager; Witaker had just accepted his third double whisky.

'And you never did find out who made the call – or why you were supposed to see Peter Gregory?'

''S'mystery, Mr Treasure. Maybe Gregory himself can

clear it up when they bring him back.' Witaker's torso
twitched again, and he glanced suspiciously behind him
for the third time in as many minutes. If the man had
been a small child Treasure would long since have told
him to stop shaking his foot in that irritating way. The
fellow was evidently a bag of nerves.

Witaker was not aware of any of these involuntary
physical aberrations. He was on his guard though – and
more than that, he was ingeniously using Treasure to
serve his own ends. British bankers invariably took things
at their face value. OK, Mr Treasure; just you retail all
this back to your important friend in Winchester's Finest.
'I sure wouldn't have left that room unless I'd been asked
– at that particular time, of course. I'd arranged to meet
the two ladies out front at firework time . . .'

'You didn't actually catch up with them?' Treasure
interjected casually, unconsciously falling into the always
infectious American idiom.

He was ready for that one. 'Well, I tried, as I told you,
but I guess I got a little mixed up in the geography. Oh,
I was there all right. I was in on that scurrilous demonstration . . . but before that, no. After the voice on the
telephone begged me to see Gregory right away – that
was, let me see, around five-forty-five – I went right over
there.' The twitch this time was more pronounced – and
he was conscious of it himself. Take another sip of Scotch;
it steadies the nerves. The only person who really knew
what was said on the telephone was the guy who made the
call – and he knew a lot. Witaker was counting on his
silence whoever he was – and counting on those photographs, those alleged photographs, never showing up.
Nobody at Itchendever had a reason any more to want to
blackmail the attorney to the Funny Farms Foundation.
There was no cause to go blabbing about threats from the
Crown Prince of Abu B'yat whether they had been true or
false – and he was beginning to believe they had been
false.

'And there was no answer when you got to Gregory's

rooms?' Treasure signalled the aged crone behind the bar whose trembling hands had so far tipped two penny-worth of lager out of each of the glasses he had ordered – another reason for the sparse attendance at The Rod and Fly. She smiled at him in return, then, as an afterthought put down her knitting and struggled over to find out what he wanted.

'None at all. I didn't go in – got to mind your manners in a strange country.' This was the second deliberate lie, but one only marginally less difficult to prove than the first.

'I don't think he could have been there at the time. It sounds as though he went into the SCR shortly after you left it.'

This was extremely useful intelligence. 'Well, I knocked on his door fit to bring the walls down.' He had been no-where near the door – or even the staircase.

'And you left the SCR by the door into the hall? Same again, please.' The old lady wiped her brow with the back of her arm and started the journey back; business was brisk tonight.

'That is so, Mr Treasure; that is exactly so.' Watch it; you're repeating yourself; take it easy on the liquor from now onwards. 'Didn't know about the door on to the terrace.' He had not known what was waiting for him outside that door either – lurking in the misty shadows. Put it out of your mind. Put the whole damn thing behind you. Forget what happened; forget those minutes – they had seemed like hours – locked in that wash-room while he shook like a leaf. His analyst had warned him a dozen times: it does no good whatsoever to dwell on these things. Look forwards, not backwards – forwards with no Amelia Hatch blotting the view; no Cyrus either. Count your blessings; if he had actually reached that staircase and knocked on the other door – that Arab prince's door – the fat would have been in the fire for sure.

'And then you just wandered around looking for Miss Stopps and Mrs Hatch?'

'That's what I told the police, Mr Treasure. It was a
fine night and I had this top-coat with me. Seemed kind
of churlish to have refused Miss Stopps's kind invitation
to take in the views. Never did find them, though – not till
the fireworks started, that is, then I was kind of cut off by
the crowd.' Safety in numbers; that's my story, Senator,
now you just try disproving it. Mr Peter Gregory is going
to witness that Common Room was empty at ten minutes
before six, so Irvine J. Witaker was absent and accounted
for – just as he was at twenty after six when all those
police cars started to arrive.

'You weren't able to follow Mrs Hatch into the hallway
when the panic started?'

Of course not you dumb idiot. 'No, sir – and that's the
unhappy part of the whole episode. I saw her up on that
raised porchway but I was down in the bleachers –
figured it'd be faster and easier to go round in back of the
Hall. I'd been standing on the car park side. That's how I
came to meet up with you when you came in through the
south entrance with Miss Stopps. I'd gotten in through
the north doorway.' And that was a pretty logical story.

For a man who had claimed earlier to be confused by
the geography of Itchendever Hall, Witaker had evidently
overcome this disadvantage in time to corroborate what he
believed to be an alibi. Treasure was coming to the conclusion that the man's guilt or innocence was something
that would need to be established by more sophisticated
means than a simple police interview or an informal chat.
Bantree was right about Witaker's apparent failure to
understand why the finger of guilt was pointing more
firmly in his direction than in any other. In what he had
told Treet and in what he had just related to Treasure, he
seemed impervious to the fact that he was offering no
witness to his alleged movements between five-forty-five
and six-thirty. Nobody so far questioned could recall
seeing Witaker between those critical times – despite the
man's insistence that he had covered most of the ground
close to the Hall, visited a staircase in the Stable Quad,

and mingled with the large crowd assembled to watch the firework display.

In Bantree's view – and Treasure had to agree – Witaker had a motive for doing away with Amelia and he could have collected the means by pocketing the dagger during the afternoon visit to Prince Faisal's rooms; as in the cases of a number of other suspects, circumstantially it could be shown that he also had the opportunity – in default of his proving otherwise, and to do that he needed witnesses.

Treasure eyed a lonely Scotch egg. This – apart from an abandoned-looking half-tomato – was the only visible justification for the plastic proclamation 'Snacks at the Bar'. The ham sandwich had been a poor substitute for dinner cooked by Audrey Bantree – a lady whom Treasure was given to describing as the only chef of his acquaintance with a medical degree. He spent a moment debating whether the Scotch egg was the last in the line due to hectic demand or merely a durable-looking, long-term survivor; the victory went to gastric discretion. Witaker followed his gaze. 'You hungry, Mr Treasure?'

'Not hungry enough.' He took out his pipe.

'I've been hungry.' This unexpected rejoinder had the ring of rueful admission – tinged with acidity: was Witaker about to become morbidly retrospective?

'After the Depression.'

He was.

'You seem to have survived.'

'It was a long time ago. My father was ruined in 1931. Killed himself. Threw himself off a building on Wall Street – ' one of the legendary army – 'I was eight years old.'

'Indeed.' There seemed to be no more suitable observation. Not for the first time, Treasure regretted that people credited him with a sympathetic disposition. It was clear, though, Witaker had abandoned the caution that had so evidently governed his attitude so far.

Witaker was no longer in any condition to govern

anything. He was overcome by a wave of exhaustion; lulled into relaxation and reflection by the liquor and the belief that he had successfully weathered an overt cross-examination. 'He married beneath him – not anyone like Mrs Hatch, you understand.' Treasure wondered whether this suggested an elevation or relegation of the late Amelia's social standing. 'My mother was on the stage.' The implication seemed clearer – but not the speaker's drift.

'So's my wife.' This was delivered brightly.

'A showgirl.' Check; it would have been stretching accuracy as well as loyalty to have pressed the similarity – even in a good cause.

'I expect she was very attractive.'

'She started in New York burlesque – and went back to it after my father died. Minsky's put me through school, Mr Treasure.'

The significance of this presumably shaming admission was entirely lost upon the banker. 'I don't know New York awfully well.' He attempted to excuse indifference with ignorance.

'Hunger and deprivation are bearable; humiliation is something else.' The maudlin mood was checked by a brief rally. 'But that's all behind me – and I owe it to Cyrus Hatch. D'you know that? Without good old Cyrus I'd still be struggling to get my shingle noticed in Pittsburgh. He was my first client . . .'

'But his patronage attracted others.' Treasure had seen the Hollywood version – several times. 'Well, probably you amply repaid him.'

''S'right. I've nothing to reproach myself for – not where Cyrus is concerned; no sir.' Witaker was warming to his subject. 'Why, d'you know . . .'

The whole episode erupted quickly and with the most staccato of warnings. The wall on which Treasure had been leaning contained a door on the other side of the bar top. Judging by the draught coming from this general area he assumed the half-glazed door led directly on to a yard, though it was too dark to be sure. He heard the door being shaken from the outside. He saw the glass slip from Witaker's hand to shatter on the metal foot-rail below the bar. The lawyer was momentarily transfixed. Then his face contorted into a mask of terror. One hand grasped at his throat, the other pointed at the door. 'Cy . . .' he gasped. He rose from the stool, swayed on his feet so that Treasure believed he was about to faint. The frightened expression gave way to one of determination. 'Cyrus!' cried Witaker at the top of his voice. 'No, it's a . . . I won't be . . .'

Apparently half-crazed – and more than half inebriated – Witaker clambered on to the bar stool and over the counter. He was frantically wrestling with the key in the door before Treasure had fully realized his intention. The old crone looked up in surprise. 'The gents is the other way,' she admonished, though judging by the customer's agitation perhaps it was as well he was getting himself outside by the fastest route. And here was another one; Treasure had launched himself over the bar. ''Arry!' she cried in the general direction of the public bar.

Treasure followed Witaker through the open door. They were in a small, badly lit courtyard walled on three sides and half-filled with a mountain of empty bottles and crates. Witaker had staggered in amongst the bottles. He was on his knees, then scrambled up again, his arms thrashing the air to maintain an uneven balance. 'He's there . . . look, he's there.' He pointed into the semi-darkness beyond the yard. Treasure could dimly discern the bent figure of a man grotesquely deformed by feet the size of tree stumps. 'After him!' Witaker was lumbering forward to the accompaniment of scattering bottles. The strange figure had been stationary; now it came to life. The silhouetted 'tree stumps' became detached. They hurtled through the air at the advancing Witaker. One caught him in the stomach, the other on the shin. The figure ahead, no longer bent, began retreating at speed. It was soon swallowed up in the darkness. Witaker was writhing in pain upon the ground. There was a brilliant flash of light, blinding in its force and suddenness. Two men appeared behind Treasure. '*Daily Express*,' said the one without the camera. 'You gents from the College, are you?'

Treasure looked down at the hapless attorney to the Funny Farms Foundation. He was lying breathless and prostrate on the ground. His body was covered in an assortment of garbage. His left foot was embedded in a bucket on the side of which a shaft of light illuminated the painted legend PIG SWILL ONLY.

CHAPTER XVI

'THE CHAP ACTUALLY thinks he's being haunted.'
Treasure turned the car on to the B3046 road posted for
New Arlesford. It was eight-thirty in the morning. He
and the Superintendent were returning to Itchendever
after an all too brief night at Bantree's home.

'Watch out for horses along here,' said the policeman
absently, while thinking of something quite different.
'Could be a sign of a guilty conscience.'

Treasure stopped the car abruptly. As though on cue,
the local riding class ambled in strength across his path.
'Nonsense – have you ever dealt with a haunted suspect
before?'

'Now you come to mention it, I don't think I have. You
got a better explanation?'

'I suppose you mean it's auto-suggestion. He thinks he's
seeing Cyrus Hatch all over the place because he's
wronged the man in some way.'

'Murdering his wife would do for starters.' An im-
maculate child on a Shetland with a sag in the middle
brought up the rear of the cavalcade. She saluted smartly
with her riding crop. This staccato action brought her
mount to an abrupt halt; it turned its head enquiringly
towards the Rolls and began breathing heavily on the
polished bonnet. 'I don't buy the bit about locking himself
in what he calls the powder-room.' Bantree was not in a
buying mood.

The Shetland relieved itself in the middle of the road,
enveloping the embarrassed child in a cloud of steam.
'Unless we can find out who kept trying the door to get in
with him.' Impervious to command as well as the first
elements of decorum, the pony turned about and carried
its protesting rider back the way they had come. Treasure

quickly set the car in motion. 'The place was supposed to be reserved for lady visitors.'

Immediately after the incident at The Rod and Fly, a thoroughly rattled and unguarded Witaker had disclosed that he had twice that evening been harassed with a visitation from the ghost of Cyrus Hatch – the first time shortly after he had left the Hall in answer to the telephone summons to see Peter Gregory: he had still managed to maintain that particular subterfuge. He insisted that Cyrus had manifested himself out of the shadows beside the north door. Seized with fright, he had rushed back into the building and shut himself in the first room to hand, closed the window and remained thus closeted for some minutes, attempting to regain his composure.

'Would you lock yourself up to get away from a ghost? I wouldn't,' asked Bantree. The point was academic since he had earlier announced a total disbelief in the existence of supernatural phenomena. 'And his reaction to the second so-called appearance was quite different – he chased after it. There's a speed trap in this village.'

Treasure had already observed the notice and dismissed the bluff it portended. Nevertheless he slowed the car to thirty miles an hour – shortly before they passed a policeman presiding over a sinister black box of equipment on the far side of an oak tree. The banker resolved to keep an open mind on the veracity of police warnings as well as the possibility of apparitions. 'Remember Witaker was with me – and in quite a different state of mind; he'd had a good deal to drink. Anyway, it wasn't a ghost that chucked those buckets at us. D'you think we'll find out who was pinching them?'

'I'm investigating a murder, not petty theft,' Bantree snorted. 'It seems everybody in Itchendever jacks up his income keeping pigs – and that includes the Vicar. According to the village copper, nicking pig food is more a local sport than a felony.'

'It may have been Miss Stopps who was trying to get into that cloakroom. Shall I ask her?' Treasure did his best to put the suggestion lightly.

'You mean am I still leaving you to confront that wily old bird about corrupting the young?' Bantree hesitated.

'I haven't told you about that officially. Look, I don't think for one minute the student demo had anything to do with the murder. Miss Stopps . . .'

'OK – she's yours for the time being. I'm going to be busy anyway, and Treet's not likely to get more out of her than you can.' Bantree acknowledged the salute of the uniformed policeman at the gate of Itchendever Hall as Treasure turned the Rolls into the drive. A number of cars were drawn up on the verge outside. 'Hm, the newspapers and the curious are here in strength. Mark, are you sure you want to go on being involved?'

'Absolutely sure. Hell, it was I who got you into it – you were supposed to be having three days off, remember? Anyway, if you're so sure about Witaker it shouldn't be long before you make an arrest, should it?' He parked the car in the same position as the day before. Bantree's was close by, where he had left it overnight.

The Superintendent made no move to get out. He looked pensive. 'I have a hunch he did it, but I'm a mile away from proving it. If I could clear up the side-shows it'd help. As I said yesterday, there were too many cooks stirring the broth. The student demo was probably incidental – but the certainty of a firework display may be key.'

'Witaker knew about the fireworks. Could he have set up the bomb scare?'

'It didn't need any setting up – all you want to start a bomb scare is a telephone. You said the students deny any knowledge of the chicken heads and the other choice cuts.'

'Yes, and since they were evidently in an unburdening mood I believe them. Are you seeing Peter Gregory again this morning?'

Bantree smiled. 'Yes, but don't worry, I won't hurt him.

I always treat millionaires with respect.'

'His girl-friend says he's refusing to touch that money.'
Treasure himself found this statement difficult to believe;
the Superintendent indicated his own incredulity with
raised eyebrows. 'What about the phone call that wasn't
mentioned in his statement?'

'That's what I'm seeing him about – to find out if he's
placed the voice.' After he had been brought back to the
College the night before Gregory had gone over his earlier
statement, remembering he had omitted to mention that
he had answered the house telephone in the SCR which
had been ringing when he entered the room. A voice had
asked for Witaker. On being told the American was not
there the caller had enquired who was speaking and
whether Gregory himself was going to watch the fireworks. The Australian had replied that he was; the telephone had then gone dead.

'It could have been Witaker himself.'

'Phoning from the Ladies . . .'

'Making sure the room was clear. Or could it have been
the person who phoned Witaker earlier, making certain
he'd left?'

'If there ever was such a call in the first place,' Bantree
put in sceptically. 'If he's cunning enough to have done
this murder then we can discount everything he's said –
including the ghostly visitations.'

'But why invent such elaborate embellishments?'

'We may not have been let into that little secret yet.
What's the betting poor dead Cyrus makes a third appearance naming the murderer.'

'Oh, come off it. You don't think he's mad enough to
think we'd . . .'

Bantree glanced at his watch. 'Your clock's slow.'
He pointed to the dashboard. 'It's also distinctly noisy – I
thought Rolls-Royce had fixed that problem,' he added
with a smirk. 'Look, most murderers are mad to some
degree, or literally mad about something – fixated,

obsessed, call it what you like. Witaker's obsessed with money – he as good as told you that last night. If shovelling that endowment into this place was in some way going to make a pauper out of the man, or his daughter, or both of 'em – he'd do everything he could to stop it. OK, there were plenty of others with a motive to oppose Mrs Hatch but you said last night that Witaker could have been robbing the old lady blind for years . . .'

'He's effectively sole Trustee; private trusts are some-times easy to manipulate. I only suggested that per-haps . . .' Professional rectitude was beginning to assert itself.

'That perhaps he's been cooking the books. Such things have been heard of even in this country.' Bantree opened the car door. 'Now I'm off – my first audience is with the celebrated Daniel Goldstein. See you later.'

Treasure smiled and nodded, but he remained seated in the car watching Bantree walk towards the Hall. Something the policeman had said struck a chord in his memory. The resulting train of thought was distasteful, but it was unavoidable – and it had nothing to do with Witaker.

The main subject of this last exchange examined himself closely in the shaving mirror provided in the guest suite bathroom. Any man would look haggard after all he had been through, even discounting yesterday's shirt and the garbage-stained suit. How much had he told Treasure? He went over the events of the night before – so far as he could remember them. Obviously they thought he was a crank – some kind of nut. In the circumstances he would have taken the same view himself if it was someone else who had been seeing ghosts. His mother had claimed to be psychic; maybe there was something to it.

Daylight helped Witaker put things in perspective. The best thing now was to get the hell out of this place – and this country. The Superintendent had said he might be needed for the inquest on Amelia – 'might be'. Did they

figure he was the murderer? He knew English law well
enough to know how to test that idea. There was nothing
that could keep him in Britain very long except a warrant.
There were some pressing reasons why he should get
home – even some he could admit to. Sorting out the
position of the Funny Farms Trust Fund qualified as a
public as well as a private reason for prompt withdrawal.
Shipping Amelia's remains back home could be handled
by others. He had ordered the hire car to take him back to
the Dorchester at noon. He reached for the airline time-
table in his briefcase.

Ribble had breakfasted early. Hunter-Smith, who was
sitting across the desk from the Dean, had managed three
hours' fitful sleep and a cup of coffee – the last taken
privately and quietly without disturbing his wife.

'Fifty thousand pounds – it's a lot of money.' The Dean
examined the cheque and the accompanying letter
addressed to the Bursar which had arrived in the morning
post. 'You say Home Counties Television is the biggest
of the commercial contractors?' He knew this already but
there were reasons why this morning he considered it
politic to defer to the Bursar's judgement.

Hunter-Smith nodded. 'HCT they're usually called. The
Senior Tutor would know more about them. *Verdict on
History* is their . . .'

'Yes, yes, quite so,' Ribble interrupted. 'It's really most
generous. You don't have trouble sleeping?'

Hunter-Smith saw no connection between the statement
and the question – nor had he yet fathomed the reason for
the Dean's changed attitude to him personally. He assumed the enquiry was kindly intended. 'I have a cough
that keeps me awake, but the College doctor . . .'

'Gives you sleeping pills, does he?' the other put in
eagerly.

'No – a cough mixture.' Ribble looked crestfallen on
receipt of this quite logical intelligence. 'Marvellous stuff,
as a matter of fact. Wasn't much use last night – too

many things on my mind.'

Ribble appeared not to be interested in cough mixture. 'No capsules – he doesn't give you capsules?' If this was a question it was clearly rhetorical. 'I expect he gives capsules to a lot of people, though.' Ribble looked up sharply. 'You don't know of anyone who gets sleeping capsules?' Hunter-Smith did not. He had expected either a heated discussion on his decision to leave UCI or a recapitulation of the shortcomings he had displayed the night before or – with luck – simply some pleased expressions on the subject of the gift. The enquiry into other people's sleeping habits and the remedies they applied was inexplicable.

'D'you take sleeping capsules, Dean?' This was intended as an innocuous enough rejoinder – even a pleasantry.

'Who wants to know?' The tone was alarmed. 'Oh – yes, I see. Sometimes. The pressures of this job – well, you know them well enough, Reginald.' He followed this with an oily smile. 'You're sure you didn't hear me call "come in" when you knocked on my door at – er – at ten to six, was it?'

'I can't be absolutely sure of the time, Dean.'

'Oh, I remember the time all right. I was in my bedder – ' the Dean was a stickler for Oxford slang; it added tone – 'getting ready to go down for the fireworks. I heard your knock – probably I didn't call out loudly enough.'

Hunter-Smith had the haziest idea of what time it had been when he slipped his letter of resignation under the Dean's door. He had admitted to knocking because it would have sounded cowardly to own that he had left the letter and run. Nor could he be aware how important it was for the Dean to establish his whereabouts around six o'clock on the previous day. When he had last interviewed Ribble, Superintendent Bantree had been giving no credence to the time of Mrs Hatch's death proffered by the police surgeon. Equally, he had been leaving nothing to chance when questioning known possessors of chlora hydrate.

'My father is returning – that means another dry day.'

Gregory smiled. 'I'll put your beer back in my fridge, Faisal. He really is a stickler for religious observance, isn't he?'

The two were drinking coffee with Fiona in the Prince's sitting-room. 'He only breaks big laws like harbouring criminals and shipping them out of the country,' laughed the girl. 'Is he angry, Faisal?' she added seriously.

'Don't think so. He sounded quite philosophical on the telephone – says he wants to see the Dean again.'

'Another take-over bid now Funny Farms have bitten the dust. I don't think it's going to work, Faisal. Anyway, I'm keeping out of his sight.' On balance Gregory reckoned the Crown Prince of Abu B'yat would probably regard him as an ingrate. The Arab attempt to rescue him from the consequences of his assumed folly had been an act of true loyalty hardly reflected in the embarrassment he had caused. He looked at the time. 'Mm, I've got to see the top copper in half an hour. Wish I could place that voice – I'm sure I've heard it before.'

'I want you to know how sorry – how sincerely sorry I am, Peter.' The young Prince looked grave. 'Apart from the misunderstanding, I should not have told the police I saw you coming out of the SCR . . .'

'Nonsense and forget it. I'd have told them myself – when I'd come round,' Gregory added with acerbity. 'At least you established I was coming out, not going in, at ten to six. Say, what were you doing at the window anyway – climbing out again?'

'How d'you mean?' asked Fiona from where she was examining the wall display of weaponry with a new interest.

'Well, the last time his father was here this young scoundrel got off an hour of meditation by retiring to the bedroom with alleged migraine, climbed out the window and joined me for a noggin – it's perfectly easy.'

'Faisal – for shame.'

The Prince disregarded Fiona's admonition. He looked seriously at Gregory. 'I give you my word, Peter, it was not like that. I didn't leave the bedroom.'

'OK, old son – I was only kidding,' said Gregory lightly.

CHAPTER XVII

THAT PART OF Itchendever village which passed for the whole in the eyes of the through traveller was something of a hoax. A few houses – mostly of late-Victorian or Edwardian vintage – straddled the road running east from Winchester. The inevitable garage of no discernible vintage whatsoever offered iced lollies, Hong Kong shirts, and cut-price tights – to disguise the fact the proprietor was having a hard time selling petrol. The Trout, though unprepossessing in itself, was a signpost to the cognoscenti. Its name and position at the junction with a narrow road leading south suggested diversion to rural and piscatorial delights beyond. The sign 'To the Church' at the same junction was more accurate in its promise. The fishing rights were sternly prescribed: the church was usually open.

Treasure was already aware that the old and aesthetically rewarding heart of the village lay down towards the river. He had decided to walk there partly for exercise and partly to avoid the confluence of sightseers waiting to observe further murders at the gates. He clambered over the perimeter railings and strode past the pub, enjoying the morning sunshine and wishing he were playing golf.

He had looked up the church in Betjeman's *Guide to English Parish Churches* before leaving London. The 'majestic seventeenth-century brick tower' could be seen from the main road. Now the 'massive buttresses to the Norman-Transitional nave' came into sight as he rounded a bend just after The Rod and Fly. He took the word of the Poet Laureate that the outside walls had been criminally wronged by being scraped of old rough-cast in 1892; even so, they still looked attractive. The Vicarage was less pleasing – at least in every aspect. The vile man who had added red-brick, bay-windowed wings to what

had clearly been a dignified mid-Georgian edifice had no
doubt been the despoiler who had soiled his hands and
mind destroying rough-cast. Not for the first time,
Treasure reflected that countless English vicarages would
now be more practical as well as seemly if Victorian
clergymen had at best been celibate and at worst obliged
to make do with three children, two servants, six bed-
rooms, and an episcopal ban on building extensions.

'Ha! Morning, my dear fellah.' The disembodied voice
of Hassock hailed from on high. The Vicar was cleaning
an upstairs window – perilously from the outside, and clad
in contrasting cassock and oilskin hat. 'Keeps the drips
off,' he shouted, squeezing a wet sponge on to the drive
with one hand while adjusting his headgear with the other.
Treasure hoped the entablature was worthy of being
treated as a boardwalk. 'Down in a jiffy; let yourself in –
the door's open.'

Treasure hesitated at the threshold. The front door was,
indeed, open wide, but two pairs of eyes were viewing him
with suspicion. Tottle, the immense black cat, was lying
just inside, absently licking the head of a fully-grown fox.
The first bizarre conclusion that Tottle might just have
captured the other animal and brought it back alive by
dint of superior force and intellect – or even sheer fright –
was dispelled as the fox rolled on to its back and began
digging the cat in the ribs with its hind legs. Tottle suffered
this distraction without removing his gaze from the new-
comer.

Though an animal lover, Treasure eschewed a first
instinct to stroke the fox for fear it might bite – and also
the cat in the reasonable certainty that it would bite. He
trod warily around both recumbent creatures into a wide
hallway arranged like a junk shop temporarily given over
to a jumble sale.

'Thought you might call; that's why we've been tidying
up the place.' Hassock, now hatless, descended the stairs
and gazed around at the confusion as though satisfied with
a job well done.

'Met Foxy Fred, have you? – tame as a Corgi, that one.' Treasure had once been bitten by a Corgi. 'Ah, I see Tottle's in from next door – Margaret must be motorizing this morning; cat gets upset in the car' – in contradistinction to the effect it had on bicycles – 'old Foxy stays indoors during the hunting season – instinct, I expect.' The Vicar picked up a tangle of blankets from the hall table, thus revealing two saucepans, a large earthenware teapot, and a toy tricycle with a missing front wheel. With a triumphant expression he grasped the teapot and replaced the blankets.

'Come and greet the happy throng.' He took Treasure by the arm and led him around a huge perambulator, full of books and an assortment of framed pictures, towards a half-open door. 'Pram belongs in the kitchen,' he remarked in passing – though whether this indicated the presence in that region of a baby, or a literate cook with a catholic taste in art, was a matter for conjecture. 'This is Mr Treasure – say hello, everybody.'

There were a dozen or more people in what probably passed as the Vicarage drawing-room – one small child was, in fact, actually engaged in proving the last point by defacing a wall with yellow chalk. An assortment of armchairs and a dilapidated sofa were arranged in a semicircle around the fireplace. These were occupied by several young men and women in dressing-gowns, reading newspapers, and an older girl in a pre-Raphaelite dress and a very pregnant condition sipping coffee from a large mug. At their feet was a gaggle of children of various ages squatting around a square piece of cardboard covered in what looked like hieroglyphics and a scatter of coloured counters. Andy, the unfortunate youth whom Treasure had encountered the day before, was kneeling amongst the children. 'My daughter, our undergraduate paying guests – but not very often, ha! – and my grandchildren, plus our friend Andy.' The Vicar introduced the throng with a proprietorial air.

'Gramps, Gramps, Andy's just got to market!' A

chubby-faced little girl screamed her important message.

'Has he now! Well done. And I've found the teapot, my cherubs.' There was a general murmur of congratulation. 'Caroline, take it out to Granny in the kitchen.' The nominated cherub hastened to obey.

'What are you playing?' asked Treasure, moving closer to the group.

'Going to Market,' chorused the children.

'It's home-made and expendable, which is just as well in this family.' The older girl had Hassock's strong chin, but her voice was soft and melodious. As if guessing the question in Treasure's mind, she added, 'They're not all mine, Mr Treasure, three of them are my sister's.'

'Saturday morning is baby-sitting time at the Vicarage,' boomed Hassock. 'Both my daughters had the good sense to settle within spitting distance.'

Treasure was examining the home-made game. 'This looks like . . .'

'Funny Farms,' put in one of the male students, languidly, and without looking up from *The Times*.

'Funny Farms my eye,' cried the Vicar. 'I was playing Going to Market in my nursery fifty years ago – you ask Margaret Stopps.'

'Pity you didn't patent it, sir – you might have been rich by now,' proffered the same young man.

'Rich? Who wants riches,' replied Hassock, scanning the threadbare carpet approvingly. 'Anyway, I didn't invent the thing, it wouldn't have been mine to patent.'

'Uncle Marcus – I got to market.' Andy, despite his disfigurement, looked somehow less conspicuous amongst this jolly, sympathetic crowd. He was dressed in a dark-coloured football jersey and blue jeans.

'I know, Andy, jolly good show.' Hassock was all encouragement. 'You've had quite a week, haven't you? Trips to town, presents, fireworks, *and* sweeping the board. Don't forget your homework now.' The lad beamed in appreciation. 'Well, Mr Treasure and I must retire to debate great issues – we'll be in my study.'

The two men threaded their way back across the hall to a small, book-lined room on the other side. Compared to what he had seen of the rest of the house, Treasure marvelled at the comparative order that reigned there. 'Devil of a mess, I'm afraid' was Hassock's unexpected comment. 'Must sort this place out one of these days. Take a pew.'

'Tell me about Andy.'

'Ha – sad case, but we're winning. He's a . . . he's a relative of Margaret Stopps. Parents killed outright in a motor crash in Rhodesia twelve years ago. Boy was in the car – badly hurt; you must have noticed that skin graft. There was some brain damage, but he's not dotty – far from it. He was in some kind of sanatorium for years making no progress to speak of. Then Margaret pulled him out and had him to live with her here. Result – a near miracle. That's devotion for you – that boy would do anything for Margaret.'

'Miss Stopps is quite old for such a responsibility . . .'

'You know, she's eighty-one – marvellous old girl. But you're quite right, she is too old – and she knows it. Two years ago Andy legally became my ward – and pupil: incidentally, young Peter Gregory helps in that connection. Andy's well past "eleven plus" standard now. He just needs time – and care. By the by, he's a grand actor – adores dressing up.' Treasure recalled the interlude when Andy's imitation of an armed soldier had been all too real. 'Margaret's settled some money on him – enough to see him through life if need be. But in my view he'll be perfectly capable of earning a living a few years from now – got a marvellous way with animals. Foxy's his pride and joy.'

'Miss Stopps is well off? I'm sorry, I didn't mean . . .'

'She's comfortably off – and she deserves it. She's had her share of troubles.'

'You've known her a long time?'

'All my life. She's not exactly local, brought up near Eastleigh, but her father and my grandfather were business partners. She was a close friend of my mother's. Wicked waste she never married – but that's another story. Was it Margaret you came to talk about?'

Treasure explained Miss Stopps's involvement in the student demonstration.

'Oh lawks,' was Hassock's first comment. 'Will the police want to see her?'

'I can't promise, but Superintendent Bantree's an understanding chap. I was planning to see Miss Stopps myself.'

'Good man. Margaret's potty about UCI, the Hall, the College – the lot. Anyone'd think the place had been *her* ancestral home. Well, it's understandable. She lived with us for a while after her own parents died – did a job of work, though. Messy one, too – unusual for a girl in those days. Anyway, she's protective about the College – doesn't want Americans and Arabs mucking it about. But I don't believe for one minute she knew what the revolting students were cooking up for last night – even if she did pay for it.'

'I believe that – and it's not all that important by itself. Without the murder the student demo would have been an internal matter.'

'I'm with you – and I see the problem. Look, Margaret's out now – probably on good works, but she's lunching with us. Could you join us? Pot luck, but you and I could have a word with her first.'

Treasure readily agreed to this proposal. 'D'you keep pigs?'

The Vicar's eyes lit up. 'Only modesty prevents me from telling you we breed nothing but champions – ha! Well one champion anyway, a Large White called Gertrude – farrowed this year. We've still got the litter – want to see 'em? Actually, Andy gets the credit.'

'And collects swill from The Rod and Fly?'

'Yes – the landlord's one of my sidesmen. He calls it his tithe. In another age, of course . . .' Hassock shrugged his shoulders. Previous generations of incumbents no doubt enjoyed the benefit of whole pigs as a right rather than mere bar scraps as a privilege from local publicans and a multitude of sinners. The Vicar looked up quizzically. 'You weren't there last night when some thugs tried roughing up Andy, were you?'

'I think I must have been one of the thugs.' Treasure explained the incident.

Hassock roared with laughter. 'Mystery solved. Andy was quite sure he was being attacked. Anyway, he's no ghost – and I can't imagine why Witaker took him for one.'

'The chap's highly strung at the moment – understandably so. He thought he'd seen a ghost through the glass door and when he got outside Andy was the only figure in sight.' Treasure did not want to enlarge on this. 'I must go. Perhaps I can see Gertrude at lunchtime.'

The two men walked to the Vicarage door where fox and cat – incongruously entwined – were enjoying a nap. 'You didn't bring your posh conveyance?'

'In deference to the cloth – it usually embarrasses my clerical friends to have a Rolls parked in their drives.'

'Ha, more misplaced socialism. I imagine it takes ten times more well-paid labour to make one of those than it does to make a Mini like mine. As a matter of fact I wanted you to let Andy sit in it. He saw it yesterday – talked about it all through breakfast.'

'Well, if he likes to meet me in the College car park at noon he can ride back here in it.' Treasure remembered the other question he wanted to put. 'Was your family the one that put the H in HTS Ltd?'

'Ha, Hassock's Prime Pork Pies and Sausages – the very same, my dear chap. You've got a good memory. Alas, they are no more – even HTS was gobbled up in a merger years ago.'

'I know, we acted for the gobblers – but you said your brother was still involved.'

'Mm, he runs one of the factories.' Hassock absently picked some blistered white paint off the front door.

'Rather him than me. Imagine having to work in a chromium-plated emporium of that sort – and most of the meat's foreign these days, too. Ha, you can't beat good old-fashioned British bangers – with any luck you'll get some for lunch.' Treasure trusted Gertrude would survive the morning. 'Everything's off the hoof in this village – Ministry-approved slaughterer just down the road.' It took a moment for the banker to appreciate that this description indicated more than a private accolade of confidence from the Vicar of Itchendever. In any case, as he set off towards the College he was too preoccupied with thoughts of Andy to be much concerned with the merits of British meat.

CHAPTER XVIII

MISS STOPPS'S ELEGANT Triumph was standing near Treasure's own car. The banker glanced about in the hope of sighting the owner. After all the trouble he had taken to protect the old lady from official admonition he was anxious she should not run into Bantree by chance. He tried the door of the car; it was open as he had expected. He scribbled a note on a sheet from the slim pad he invariably carried with him and tried to prop it against the steering-wheel. Since it refused to remain propped, he searched around inside the car for some implement to hold it in position. A piece of Sellotape attached to a transparent plastic package was easily detached and provided precisely what he needed. He replaced the package in the glove pocket where he had found it – and where Miss Stopps had probably forgotten it. He made a mental note to mention its existence to her – for Miss Stopps was not the type of citizen who would ignore a parking fine demand and risk sterner retribution from the City of London Police.

'Mr Treasure – if we might have a word.' The probability that they would have several was confirmed as Treasure turned to discover that it was indeed Ribble who had uttered and who was now bobbing about nervously beside him. 'You may be aware that I am under suspicion.' Personal predicament was evidently taking precedence over official preoccupation with the disciplining of unruly students – or even a show of responsible anguish at the unwelcome addition of murder to extra-curricular activities.

'On the contrary, Dean, I find that impossible to credit.'

Ribble mopped his brow, despite the crisp November temperature. 'Last evening I was questioned most exhaustively by the Inspector . . .'

'So were lots of other people. Have you seen Superintendent Bantree this morning?'

'No, but I fear that is an ordeal to come. You see, I was in possession of sleeping capsules . . .'

'But not enough to have done any harm to Mrs Hatch.' Treasure saw no reason to withhold what in any case he did not regard as a confidence. Ribble stopped hopping. 'I gather you handed over the capsules you had left to the Inspector.'

'The bottle was half empty.'

'Then you should know your doctor's confirmed he's only once prescribed you chloral hydrate and that the quantity imbibed by Mrs Hatch indicates the concentration in the bottle of rum was far too strong to have been squeezed out of your little supply.' The Dean was all attention. 'I'm surprised the Inspector hasn't told you.'

The relief was evident in Ribble's expression – but it was not complete. 'I was also asked to account for my movements between certain times.'

'And you couldn't – neither can most other people. Unfortunate, but there it is. I don't imagine they're crediting you with a motive for doing in Mrs Hatch so if I were you I'd relax.'

'That, I fear, is out of the question, but I'm most grateful for your view. My concern for the College, its reputation, and so on, believe me, transcends any worry about my own position – but the two things are interlocked, as you must see. We cannot afford a scandal – I mean of course, a worse scandal. The involvement of someone such as myself even as a temporary suspect, if it got out . . .'

'Would be as unfortunate as it is unlikely.' Treasure tried to invest this almost unsupported pronouncement with the authority of one who enjoyed the complete confidence of all concerned in the investigation – possibly from the Home Secretary downwards. In mitigation he was well aware of Bantree's view that Eric Ribble failed dismally to qualify as the likely perpetrator of a fairly sophisticated crime – on grounds of competence. While he could hardly share this at once unflattering if reassuring opinion with the Dean, he saw no harm in predicating its effect. In any case, he required the man's full attention in another context. 'In other words, old chap, I'd stop worrying.' Ribble seemed partially mollified as Treasure continued. 'Now that the Funny Farms endowment is down the drain, what about the College finances?' Lord Grenwood was less likely to be concerned with murder most foul than he would be with the news that his pet charity was once more heading for the rocks.

'Ah, there, at least, we have an encouraging development.' Treasure hoped this did not presage an assumption on Ribble's part that following embarrassment as well as insult the Crown Prince of Abu B'yat would still be disposed to shower riches on UCI. 'This morning we received a donation of fifty thousand pounds – the first of three such promised over the next two years.'

'Anonymous?' Treasure glanced involuntarily at the expensive Triumph.

'The money comes as a charitable donation from Home Counties Television. It would be naïve to assume that so commercial a body has been wholly motivated by feelings of simple generosity.' Ribble rallied to the extent of a half smile. 'The Bursar takes the view that we are indebted to Daniel Goldstein for the gift.'

'And I'm inclined to agree with him.' Based on the quite substantial sums Treasure himself received for occasional and often fleeting appearances on television, he calculated that the figure mentioned might equate with the annual retainer Goldstein could demand in return for contracting his services to the television company on an exclusive basis. He called to mind reading that *Verdict on History* had been sold by HCT to television stations in various parts of the English-speaking world. 'Have you asked Goldstein about it?'

'Unfortunately he was closeted with the police earlier on and he is now conducting a tutorial.' The last information at least indicated that the Senior Tutor had so far avoided arrest.

Ribble adopted a philosophical tone as the two men made their way towards the College at Treasure's instigation. 'I have thought a good deal about the wisdom of accepting the Funny Farms endowment – ' most particularly since the opportunity of doing so had evaporated – 'and I have concluded we may have been misguided in our enthusiasm. There still exists, of course, the possibility of some accommodation with Sheikh Al Haban – ' but, thanks to Daniel Goldstein, on terms that would not involve the Arabs taking over the establishment. Treasure believed he understood Ribble's drift. If the Dean could be judged too incompetent to commit murder, his pragmatic approach to finance offered earnest of his capacity as a horse-trader. A quarter of a million pounds from Al Haban, plus a hundred and fifty thousand from HCT would be more than sufficient to keep the College out of the red for the foreseeable future as well as to pay for some modest capital improvements. Even without Arab funds – and UCI's new obligation to the Senior Tutor might preclude their acceptance – the television money would at least underwrite the survival of the institution for some while to come.

The last conclusion invented a question in Treasure's mind. 'D'you suppose the anonymous gift received earlier this year . . .'

'Was also a gift from Daniel?' Ribble broke in. He continued with a nod. 'That is the Bursar's view, and I am inclined to agree. Daniel himself will never admit it, of course – I doubt, even, he will confirm his responsibility for the fresh munificence.' Which, thought Treasure, would also preclude the HCT money being used by Goldstein as a reason for turning down an Arab deal. As though following the same train of thought Ribble added, 'Daniel is a strange man with a rigidly stern set of values. It would not be in his nature to use his generosity to sway our decisions.' He stopped to face Treasure as the two men

reached the steps to the Hall portico. 'If Mrs Hatch had
not been murdered we should this morning have been
completing arrangements to accept her endowment. We
should none the less have received the quite unconditional
gift from the television people – it was posted yesterday
morning. Daniel would still have been relying on the
force of his own personality to prevent what he regarded
as my persistence in error. A strange man, Mr Treasure,
and an intellectually honest one – ruthless in many ways,
but . . .'

Ribble shook his head. He left the sentence uncom-
pleted, and Treasure to the reflection that ruthlessness
could manifest itself in a variety of ways.

'What did I tell you?' Bantree announced smugly as
Treasure entered the Bursar's Office. 'The full weight of
the medical evidence has dropped with a dull thud. Time
of death? Anywhere between five-forty-five and six-
forty-five.' He waved some sheets of paper in the air. 'So
they're not telling us much we don't know already. She
was done in after six-twelve, which is the last time anyone
saw her. Why this medico persists in extending the period
backwards heaven knows.' He read from the typewritten
report. ' "Professional integrity" my foot – professional
conceit more likely. Anyway, the Dean's off the hook. He
was remonstrating with some students outside the JCR
at fire-cracker time, and half a dozen people remember
seeing him throughout the stirring events afterwards.
Same goes for the drunken Bursar. Help yourself to a cup
of coffee. Your friend Goldstein's a deep one.'

Treasure paused before pouring the liquid from the
Thermos jug in his hand. 'D'you suspect him?'

'Of setting up diversions, muddying the waters, and
making life difficult for honest policemen – yes. Of murder
– frankly I don't know. Oh, he's capable of it – he as good
as said so. Mrs Hatch was misguided – he's outraged at the
manner of her leaving – but he's not sorry she's gone. Like

some Counter-Reformation Jesuit justifying a religious execution.'

'And where was he during the critical hour?'

'In his study listening to Bach.'

'Well, he can't be all bad. I can add a little in terms of character reference.' Treasure went on to relate the details of the gift from HCT. 'Of course,' he ended, 'we can't know for sure that the manna was arranged by Goldstein – and Ribble doubts he's going to admit to it – but I know the Chairman of HCT: he's not noted for giving the company's money away.'

'The whole thing could be another diversion. Incidentally, Goldstein's no more fond of the Arabs than he is of the Funny Farms bunch – he made that quite plain – and if he didn't set up the bomb scare I'll bet he wished he had.'

'You think he did?'

'Almost certainly. He gave it away in his eyes when I told him the Sheikh was on his way back. Obviously he thought the Middle Eastern contingent had been wiped off the board.'

'But Al Haban is returning to treat? I thought he might be from something Ribble said. You'd better have that helicopter standing by.' Treasure paused. 'Could Goldstein have doctored the rum?'

'If he was lurking in the Common Room waiting for Mrs Hatch to put in her exclusive appearance – yes. His wife's had enough chloral hydrate prescribed over the last two years to lace a distillery – but then, so has the Vicar, and half the village, as we discovered after more exhaustive enquiry from the open-handed doctor.' Bantree's opinion of the medical profession was deteriorating by the hour. 'Mark you, Mrs Goldstein swears she uses the stuff regularly – Treet interviewed her this morning. Incidentally, the knock-out drops introduce another medical inconsistency. Our quack insists that if he can't be certain about the time of death, he's absolutely certain that the drug was swallowed twenty minutes before –

something to do with the way it disperses.'

'Perhaps Amelia packed a hip flask – she certainly pre-dated Prohibition.'

'I thought of that, but there's no flask amongst her effects over there.' Bantree nodded at the small table where the contents of Mrs Hatch's handbag were neatly arranged. Treasure moved across the room to inspect them. 'The only time we know she took a drink was at five-thirty.'

'Which fits with your surgeon's theory about the earliest time of death.'

'Not necessarily. She could have had another drink with the drug in it later – or she could have taken chloral hydrate by itself to calm her nerves at six-fifteen. The alcohol and the drug weren't necessarily taken at the same time – only probably.'

'They were in the case of Peter Gregory, which suggests . . .'

'She nicked the bottle or filled a flask from it – or went back for a quick one before the fireworks. I'm going to have to see Miss Stopps. What did you get out of her this morning?'

Treasure explained his failure to track down the lady, but in compensation he was able to clear up the mystery of the disappearing pig swill.

Bantree was not much interested in pigs. 'If Miss Stopps is here now, I'll have someone find her. She told Treet they never came into the building again – she and Mrs Hatch, I mean – after they left at five-thirty. He didn't ask her whether the old girl had another drink outside.'

'Is it all right to touch these things?' Treasure indicated the handbag contents.

'Sure,' said Bantree. He looked across at Treasure. 'We still haven't found the hat and coat – or a scarf that belonged to Miss Stopps.'

Treasure was examining a wallet. 'Amelia hated taking her coat off . . . Good Lord!' He was staring at a faded photograph of a very old man. It was housed behind a piece of transparent plastic on the inside of the wallet.

'What have you found?'

'I'm not sure.' The likeness was remarkable. 'Have you seen Witaker this morning?'

'Yes – and better acquaintance doesn't endear. I've got a copper's hunch about that one. He's sticking to his story, and while he can't prove it with witnesses, I can't disprove it. The Pittsburgh police have seen his doctor who confirms he's never had chloral hydrate prescribed – for what that's worth. It doesn't mean he didn't get some here, of course.'

Treasure interrupted. 'But from what Treet gleaned from Miss Stopps, Witaker was nowhere near the rum bottle from the time it was brought in to the time Amelia helped herself.'

'But he had plenty of opportunity to lace it afterwards – so if she took a slug later . . .'

'He wouldn't have had time to cut her throat. Remember he was with me in the hall just after the helicopter arrived.'

'What if she had the second drink at six – as Witaker might have figured she would. He follows her into the Common Room after the fireworks, locks the door, kills her, arranges the suicide scene . . .'

'And leaves by the terrace, taking her hat and coat with him – for no reason that's clear unless he thinks people usually take off their outdoor clothes before committing suicide. But what did he do with the hat and coat – drop 'em in a dustbin?'

Bantree shook his head. 'Every kind of receptacle was searched last night. But it's all possible, Mark – the hat and coat aren't that important.' He picked up the internal telephone and dialled a number. 'Bantree here. Miss Margaret Stopps is somewhere on the premises. I want to see her now – give it top priority.' He replaced the receiver. 'At least we can find out if Mrs Hatch was out of Miss Stopps's sight at any point.'

'She's already said she wasn't.'

'Yes, but she might not count going to the loo, for instance – and that cloakroom Witaker claims he hid in is right next to the Common Room and the north entrance to the Hall.' Bantree drummed the desk with his fingers. 'Witaker wants to leave at midday and he's taking a plane to the States at five.'

'You can hold him for questioning . . .'

'But not indefinitely, and unless something turns up . . .'

As though on cue, a knock at the door heralded the appearance of the ample Inspector Treet. He nodded at Treasure, then turned to Bantree. 'Somebody at the lab gets E for effort, sir. Some of those drinking-glass fragments we collected from the porch last night held traces of rum and chloral hydrate. Oh, and I gather you wanted to see Miss Stopps in a hurry. I'm afraid she left a few minutes ago – she passed the time of day with the local bobby – told him she was going to market. Shall I have her fetched back?'

Although it was following these words that the pieces seemed to fall into place for Treasure, they were not yet in a neat enough pattern for displaying to Bantree: 'Colin, will you tell Witaker he can leave for town at noon?' he asked slowly. 'I want to run into him as he's leaving – outside, and off his guard. If he thinks you're letting him go, then he will be.'

Bantree gave his friend a quizzical look. 'Solved the crime that has the coppers baffled, have we? Tell me more.'

'On condition you keep your promise to let me have first go at Miss Stopps.'

The Superintendent agreed.

CHAPTER XIX

'FLY – ALL IS discovered,' said the singsong voice on the house telephone.

'Who is it, for God's sake?' Witaker's unguarded, fearful reaction to the disquieting injunction was well above average, even for a professional man.

'Call it your conscience.' This was followed by some heavy breathing. 'Before you go, though, we want you to make a promise to the Dean. You must tell him that you will arrange a donation of half a million dollars from your funny foundation to the College – provided he accepts no money from the Arabs.'

'I have no authority . . .'

'We know that, you blithering idiot. All you need do is make the promise – otherwise those candid camera shots will receive the widest possible advertisement. Come, we are not asking much of you in return for peace and comfort. We know far more than you think. I repeat, *all* has been discovered.'

'Can I have the photographs . . . and the negatives?'

'They will be destroyed – you have our word on it, and we are honourable men. If we were not, don't you think we'd be asking for more than a mere promise? Think what you're getting away with, Witaker – think hard.'

There was no point in holding on to the receiver; the line had gone dead.

Witaker fumbled in his pocket for the pill box, then stumbled to the bathroom for a glass of water. He had closeted himself in the guest suite to avoid people and publicity while he waited for official permission to leave. As he swallowed the third tranquillizer of the morning there was a loud knock on the bedroom door. Although this increased his sense of impending doom, in fact it announced the arrival of a messenger from Bantree to say he could go when he chose.

In another part of the College, the Senior Tutor sat back with a satisfied air. 'You don't think I overdid the Pakistani accent?'

'I thought it was meant to be Welsh.' Peter Gregory smirked at his celebrated friend.

'The difference in the cadences might not be perceived by a Colonial such as yourself.' Goldstein was sensitive about his abilities as a mimic.

'D'you think he'll play?'

'If he's as crooked as I think he is – he'll co-operate. What has he got to lose? He makes the promise, which by itself puts Ribble in a hell of a spot. Witaker thinks he'll have to explain later that the Funny Farms Trustees or beneficiaries won't play . . .'

'By which time I shall have established my right to a tenth of the loot – half of which I'll give to the College.' Gregory had reached a compromise on scruple and adopted a plan that satisfied his conscience and funded his future with Fiona.

'Mm, I wouldn't be in too much of a hurry on that. I imagine friend Witaker may have more exploitable good-will than even he credits with the other nine grateful beneficiaries. If he makes a public promise they may well feel obliged to make it stick, assuming he gets out of this scot free – especially if the tenth recipient – that's you, my boy – presses the point. Anyway, the main thing is to have him throw our Eric off balance before he confronts the Arab League.'

'If five million adoring viewers knew what a Machiavellian character you are . . .'

'It would endear them to me even more,' Goldstein observed loftily. 'Your allusion is, in any case, inapposite. Machiavelli never used the telephone; it wasn't invented. Even so, I doubt he could have employed it to better effect if I say so myself. I retract any aspersion on your perception.'

'The bomb scare was going a bit far.'

Goldstein's large frame shook with silent laughter. 'How was I to know they'd bring in the ruddy armed forces? I thought Al Haban would just send down his bodyguards to have a look-see – I'm sure he regards them as expendable.'

'You're not kidding about that other phone call to the SCR – the one I took?'

'There are limits to my perfidy – even in a good cause. I repeat, it was not I. Anyway, you'd have recognized me by whatever phoney accent I adopted.' The Senior Tutor was getting his own back.

'There was no discernible accent – and I'm still sure I've heard the voice before.' Gregory pondered the point, then shrugged his shoulders. 'What are you going to do with the photographs? Can I see them?'

'Shame on you – and your vulgar, salacious curiosity. I shall destroy them as I promised. They are two in number incidentally. One of Witaker going into a Euston brothel and another of him coming out. The private investigator I employed to dog the footsteps of the late Mrs Hatch and her lackey had neither the initiative nor the influence to produce anything more damning.'

'You old fraud.'

'Not at all.' Goldstein effected an expression of offended innocence. 'Anyway, hiring the private eye was a brilliant stroke. If he hadn't tipped off the newspapers about the Funny Farms story and the whereabouts of Mrs Hatch our cause would have enjoyed a good deal less celebrity and support, don't you think?'

Gregory nodded. 'Faisal says his father is going to move heaven and earth to get in, now the other business is over.'

'But the "other business", as you call it, had a good deal of support. Charming as your pupil may be, there are few here who want his family to be exerting undue influence in our affairs. The elimination of the Arabs should cause us a good deal less trouble than Mrs Hatch.'

'D'you still think Witaker is the murderer?'

'Let's just say I hope he isn't so careless as to get himself arrested before our worthy Dean accepts his promise and sees off Al Haban.'

At a few minutes before twelve, Witaker and Ribble came down the steps of Itchendever Hall deeply engaged in conversation. The Bursar was bringing up the rear, but at a discreet distance. Treasure watched them approaching him in the car park area. He was standing between his own car and the hired Daimler which had arrived to collect Witaker. The engine of the Rolls was running on a rich mixture. As a result, fusion of the exhaust fumes with the chill outside air produced a foul-smelling fog that virtually enveloped the car. As Treasure had earlier observed, similar if lower horse-powered effects could be obtained with the exudations of Shetland ponies. The Daimler driver cast a disapproving glance in Treasure's direction, considered moving his vehicle, but on catching sight of his passenger decided to endure the affront to his lungs for the moments that remained before he could depart.

Treasure stepped forward. 'So, you're leaving?'

Witaker, crumpled and bowed, gave a short nod. 'The Superintendent doesn't need me any more.' There was less satisfaction in the voice than might have been expected.

Ribble, at least, seemed to have recovered his normal bounce. 'Mr Witaker has made us a most generous promise . . . indeed, in the circumstances, a most magnificent promise.'

'I can't guarantee anything . . .'

The Dean smiled warmly. 'He naturally cannot commit his new fellow Trustees to the Funny Farms Foundation, but he has promised to use his influence to obtain an Amelia Hatch memorial donation to UCI – the figure of half a million dollars has been mentioned.'

Treasure nodded approvingly at this unexpected, and

in the circumstances, inappropriate intention. The form
of Amelia's passing hardly justified memorizing. 'I
sincerely hope you can push it through.' He glanced about
him as though conscious for the first time of the clouds of
smoke engulfing the party. 'I say, I'm sorry about the fug.
Hang on a second.'

Treasure hurried around his car to the driver's door,
and thrusting his hand through the open window, switched
off the ignition. Witaker was standing near the front
passenger door of the Rolls as the exhaust haze began to
disperse on the light breeze.

'I think you've met my passenger.' Treasure addressed
Witaker over the roof of the car. Andy was sitting in the
front seat; his face appeared, wraith-like, through the
wafted smoke. Witaker stared at the boy in frightened
disbelief. All colour drained from his face. His mouth
opened, but no words emerged. 'Spitting image, isn't he?'
continued Treasure jauntily. 'But you haven't been seeing
ghosts, old chap – this is Andy Stopps, a lad who lives here
in the village.' He walked around the car and proffered
his hand to Witaker. 'Well, in case I don't see you again,
cheerio, and a safe journey.' He looked over Witaker's
shoulder. 'Hello, Colin, you look very purposeful.'

Superintendent Bantree had joined the group. He
motioned Witaker towards the rear of the Daimler. 'If we
could have a word alone, sir. Excuse us, gentlemen.'

Ribble and the Bursar remained where they were
standing, looking decidedly perplexed. What had taken
place had all the appearances of a set piece, and it was
disquieting to have been unrehearsed participants.

After a moment's hesitation Hunter-Smith followed
Treasure who, after a nod to the Dean, was ambling un-
concernedly back to his car. 'Mr Treasure.' The Bursar
spoke in a near whisper. 'Something I should have
mentioned to the police perhaps.' He nodded towards the
lonely passenger in the Rolls. 'Bad form to get a lad like
that into trouble unnecessarily – may be nothing in it,
too – leave you to be the judge, what? Fact of the matter

is, I saw young Andy there hanging about outside the
SCR – that is, on the terrace – just before the fireworks
started last night.' He gave a short sigh as though to
indicate he was glad to have relieved himself of a responsibility – even if it was one he owed to his wife's insistence
rather than to his own conscience.

'I think you'll find the police have that information
already. Anyway, I should certainly let Inspector Treet
know what you've told me. Can you remember the exact
time you saw Andy?'

The Bursar looked embarrassed. 'You probably know
I'd had a few – no, I can't be exactly sure of the time. It
must have been four or five minutes before the fireworks
started.' He paused. 'Well, if you feel I ought to speak up.'
Hunter-Smith wheeled about, military style, and marched
back to rejoin the deserted Ribble.

Treasure headed the car for the village glancing from
time to time at the boy sitting beside him so obviously
overwhelmed and delighted by the ride. The Bursar's
sentiments were clearly the right ones. Andy deserved as
much protection as Treasure or anyone else could provide.
Fate had dealt him some bitter blows – his disfigurement
and retarded mental development were proof of that. If
Treasure's hypothesis was correct – and he now had no
doubt that it was – a stubborn if understandable sense of
respectability and pride had deprived the boy of vast
riches: of course, love and care had been provided in
ample compensation, and it was interesting to speculate
on the possibility that the riches were still not beyond
claiming. For the moment, however, there was a consideration that took priority over all material matters.
Through a misguided application of rough justice Andy
stood in danger of being arraigned as an accessory to
murder.

Miss Stopps was arranging herself to mount the bicycle
after pushing it up the hill to The Trout. Tottle settled
himself more comfortably – as forward look-out – while

marking the progress of the Rolls. Instead of descending
the hill, Treasure steered the car to the side of the road,
and stopped.

'Auntie, Auntie, look at me!' Andy called through the
open door as Treasure alighted.

The banker turned. 'Andy, why don't you run on down
and tell Uncle Marcus I'll be there shortly – you can be
getting Gertrude ready for showing, and you can come for
another ride with me later.' The first look of disappointment was replaced by one of eagerness at the last promise.
Treasure joined Miss Stopps on the far side of the road as
Andy jogged away towards the village.

'He's a great credit to you.'

'One does one's best, Mr Treasure. Now I fear I am far
too decrepit and useless . . .'

'The Vicar explained. I'm sure no . . . no grandmother
could have done more.' Treasure offered the title so that it
might have been construed as a convenient simile. Miss
Stopps displayed no visible reaction. 'Mr Witaker was
much taken with Andy's likeness to someone else. It quite
unnerved the poor chap.'

'How very strange and . . .'

'Unexpected? Perhaps. Witaker insists that Andy's the
living image of Cyrus Hatch. The old chap was quite bald
apparently – that was, in his later years.'

'Indeed.' Miss Stopps gave no more than a well-
mannered show of interest. Other people's coincidences,
she might have been indicating, were on a par with other
people's dreams as subjects for third-party fascination.
'Mr Treasure, I haven't thanked you for your note – most
thoughtful. I took your advice and left the College immediately.'

'I'd assumed . . .'

'That I should be awaiting you at my cottage?' Miss
Stopps interrupted, and, after consulting her watch, continued. 'You are a trifle earlier than I had expected, so
having put our house in order, Tottle and I decided on a
quick spin.' She paused. 'The possibility that Mrs Hatch

committed suicide has been ruled out?'

'That will depend on the inquest.'

'Quite so. For my own part I had judged appearances would indicate suicide.'

'The post-mortem showed large quantities of a soporific drug in the body – chloral hydrate. The police have concluded Mrs Hatch was unconscious when her . . . when the dagger was used.'

Miss Stopps nodded. 'I know the substance. Marcus has it prescribed – I borrow some from time to time, I must confess, often without his knowledge. The Hassocks keep a commendably open house.' She waited long enough to ensure these last remarks had registered before continuing. 'The authorities are very conscientious.'

'You mean confronted with such obvious evidence of suicide one wouldn't have expected them to dig any deeper? They're usually pretty thorough in these matters – and the circumstances were odd.'

'Amelia confided in me that she had an inoperable form of cancer – perhaps the post-mortem revealed as much?' Treasure nodded gravely. Miss Stopps continued. 'She feared a protracted illness. Suicide is not uncommon in such cases – the drug might have been taken to make her resolve easier to . . . to execute.'

'That would have been an entirely likely conclusion if she hadn't taken so much. Indeed, if her throat hadn't been cut, I understand the dose might have proved lethal by itself.'

'It would?' It was difficult to tell whether there was more of disappointment than curious dismay in the expression.

'Mm, and if she'd died in that way suicide would have been the likeliest verdict.' Miss Stopps accepted this information with an audible sigh. 'If, though, as you suggest, the drug was to make things easier for an elderly lady to complete her purpose – ' Treasure's eyes met those of Miss Stopps – 'then I'm afraid the thing badly misfired.'

'Because it made suicide impossible.' Miss Stopps

stroked Tottle's head: she examined features of the landscape surrounding the pair as though viewing them for the
first time; then, without looking at Treasure, she continued. 'The police do not assume that there was more
than one person involved?'

'That depends on whether they catch their murderer,
whether he . . . whether he or she makes a full confession,
and whether it's apparent that any accomplice or ac-
complices served that role wittingly or unwittingly.'

'And do you believe they will catch their murderer?'

'I think they're very close.'

Miss Stopps assumed a determined expression. 'Then we
must do what we can to ease the course of justice, Mr
Treasure. Yes, we must all do what we can.' The banker
recalled hearing those same words from those same lips
just twenty-four hours before. 'Well, Marcus will be waiting for us.' She glanced at the cat. 'Time's up, Tottle.'

Treasure recrossed the side road to his car. It was the
throb of a powerful engine that caused him to glance back
– half protectively, half expecting to see Miss Stopps
safely beginning her free-wheel descent towards the
Vicarage. He was thus in time to watch a sequence of
events he was never to forget.

The main road had been empty – and was so still –
excepting only for a heavy articulated lorry which had
suddenly appeared moving at speed in the direction of
Winchester. Without warning, Miss Stopps launched her
cycle not down the hill but straight under the nearside
front wheel of the giant vehicle's second container
section. There was no time for the driver to swerve – no
opportunity for him to endanger himself; no other road
users at risk. All this Miss Stopps had had time to gauge,
and it was characteristic that no doubt she had done so.
The driver felt the impact, then saw it through his wing
mirror. He braked hard, but to no purpose. Bicycle and
rider had been tossed aside and into the air with tremendous force. Treasure raced towards the recumbent body at
the roadside; it was predictably lifeless.

'You saw what 'appened, mate?' The lorry driver was at Treasure's side as he stood up from examining Miss Stopps's body. The banker nodded. 'Thank Gawd for that. Is she mad or somethin'?'

'In some respects, yes.' Treasure spoke almost to himself, then, glancing at the driver he added in a firmer tone, 'I think the cat must have upset her intentions.'

Tottle, ruffled but unharmed, treated Treasure to a malevolent glare.

CHAPTER XX

IT WAS TWO hours later: Bantree looked up from reading the letter in his hand. 'It's a plain enough confession, and it certainly clears the boy – but why in the world did she do it?' He glanced from Treasure to Hassock in search of enlightenment. The three were seated in the Vicarage study.

'An intense love, a burgeoning hatred – and a one in a million coincidence that made the mix combustible.'

'I think Treasure's got it right,' Hassock volunteered. 'I just wish I'd seen it coming.'

'You couldn't have – oh, you knew about Going to Market being similar to Funny Farms and you knew about Miss Stopps's illegitimate child. You didn't know that Cyrus Hatch had been the father.'

'I knew whoever it was had jilted Margaret in 1919. Being an unmarried mother wasn't funny in those days, either.'

'All of us had some of the facts,' Treasure continued, 'but I was the only one who saw the look on Witaker's face when he caught sight of Andy.'

Bantree nodded. 'Judging from the photo, at first glance Andy really does seem to be a reincarnation of Hatch.'

'More so than Andy's father, as a matter of fact,' put in Hassock. 'We grew up together of course. He emigrated after the war. Likenesses sometimes do skip a generation and, there again, Andy's father didn't last long enough to go bald. Ha, more's the pity.'

'So putting the pieces together?' Bantree had the solution to the crime; he was still not sure about the motive.

'Putting the pieces together,' said Treasure, 'Hatch was billeted on Miss Stopps's family at Bishop's Oak. Not only does he seduce and jilt the daughter, but later he makes a fortune from a commercial version of the Stopps family's board game.'

'Ha! Meantime Margaret's ostracized by her own people and she and her son are taken in by my dear old mother, bless her compassionate heart. The family upset didn't last long because old Stopps died in 'twenty-two, and Margaret inherited the business.' The Vicar glanced up at Treasure. 'It was the Stopps who put the S in HTS Ltd when we amalgamated. The Stopps slaughterhouses were a key part of what my brother would call an inter-dependent conglomerate – we converted meat from off the hoof to processed foods.'

'Cyrus Hatch seems to have caused Margaret Stopps a good deal of insult and injury – but she bore it all without complaint, or, it would appear, thought of revenge or recrimination.' Treasure looked to Hassock for confirmation.

'Ha, absolutely. She immersed herself in the business – built it up, as a matter of fact . . .'

'So she was no stranger to slaughter,' put in Bantree.

'Not of animals, certainly. It was a messier business in those days, too – and, I suppose, a good deal less humane than it is now.' Hassock paused to reflect. 'Margaret was completely bound up in her work and in her son. Then, suddenly she had neither – the business was sold, her son had been killed.'

'But her grandson, Andy, and UCI replaced them?' It was Treasure who put the question.

'Ha, absolutely. She had enormous energy and the strongest sense of service I've ever come across. I don't think it's an overstatement to say the College would have gone under without her involvement.'

'And then, along comes this woman who pinched her lover threatening to take the place over,' Bantree added quickly.

'That's how it could have looked to Margaret, certainly,' the Vicar agreed.

'But murder?'

'Was a last, not a first resort.' Treasure pressed his assertion. 'The gory warnings might have done the trick. Incidentally, I think you'll find they came from the local abattoir. I gather Miss Stopps had the run of the place . . .'

Hassock nodded vigorously. 'The manager's an old friend and Margaret used to work wonders with offal – marvellous cook. She was always there helping herself to bits and pieces.' Bantree made a note, though more out of habit than necessity.

'Andy delivered the boxes when Miss Stopps gave him an outing in London on Thursday.' Treasure glanced at the Superintendent. 'Of course, he didn't know what was in them, and probably Miss Stopps left the car and hovered in the background to make sure he didn't get into any trouble with porters or doormen. She got a parking ticket a street away from my office. I didn't twig its significance when I first saw it. The chicken heads may have been a last-minute touch, but they'd have been easy enough to secrete in that bag of hers. She must have strung them to the taps in the washroom before she joined the crowd in the SCR.'

'But it's a big jump from issuing warnings to committing murder.' Bantree sounded official.

'Perhaps in contemplation but not when it comes to the point.' Treasure hesitated. 'Before she'd met Mrs Hatch I believe Miss Stopps might have been committed to nothing more than the warnings and the student demonstration – but I believe she'd decided on sterner measures before the end of the afternoon. If Hassock here is right about the degree of her devotion to the College it must have been unendurable to sit at that meeting listening to the woman who had in effect stolen the man in her life making arrangements to steal the institution that . . .'

'Had filled the emotional vacuum.' Bantree was beginning to understand.

'Amelia Hatch had a certain comic quality for me. To

Margaret Stopps . . .'

'She'd have been a slap in the face with a wet fish.' It
was Hassock who offered the apposite analogy.

Treasure gave the slightest smile. 'A terrible shock and,
if you like, the final insult. And after Miss Stopps had done
everything in her power to dissuade Mrs Hatch from endowing the College, I believe she went home to improve
on the vague murder plan that had been forming in her
mind.'

'Improve on it?' Both men looked surprised; it was
Bantree who put the question.

'Yes. She'd seen Mrs Hatch drinking rum before lunch.
But for that I believe Miss Stopps would simply have
dropped the chloral hydrate into the victim's tea in the
hope that the taste wouldn't be detected and that the dose
would have been lethal. Trouble was, she wasn't sure
whether the stuff would kill or not.'

'It would have in a big enough quantity, taking her age
and condition into account,' said Bantree. 'Mark you, it
would have made murder more obvious – and the
murderer.'

'Not at all, Colin.' Treasure lit the pipe he had been
filling. 'Miss Stopps could have told us afterwards that
Mrs Hatch had mentioned taking a soporific – according
to Witaker, they both had a short nap after tea. My guess
is that if that plan had been followed we'd all have
assumed Mrs Hatch took an overdose by mistake.'

'Assuming she'd drunk the tea; it would have tasted
foul,' said Bantree.

'That was the obvious weakness,' Treasure agreed.
'Otherwise I'm sure you'd have taken Miss Stopps's word,
and I've no doubt she might have planned to drop a few
chloral hydrate capsules into the victim's handbag to
make it all seem authentic. But the rum changed the plan
– that and the cat.'

'Tottle?' Hassock looked up in surprise.

Treasure nodded. 'Miss Stopps arrived by bike yesterday morning with her cat. I'm sure this indicated she

didn't expect to be staying all day – and she was certainly hoping that Mrs Hatch wouldn't show up at all after the warnings. She couldn't have known that if Mrs Hatch came after all then the decision about the endowment would have been made so quickly – hence the arrangement of the student protest. Miss Stopps had no intention of being a witness to that protest. You don't take a cat to a firework display.'

'Nor chloral hydrate to a tea-party.' The cynical aside was Bantree's.

'She may or may not have had that with her in the morning. What she certainly didn't have was a conveyance in which to hide and spirit away Amelia's coat and hat – if that became necessary.'

'I don't understand,' said Hassock. Bantree was in the same condition but he had no intention of admitting it.

Treasure's brow furrowed as he concentrated. 'The scenario, as I see it, went like this. Miss Stopps poured the chloral hydrate into the rum soon after the bottle was brought in after tea. Witaker was on the other side of the room; so was Mrs Hatch, taking her nap. Miss Stopps was prepared to offer Mrs Hatch a snifter to keep her warm before they went out, but she didn't have to. The sight of the bottle was enough for Amelia. Miss Stopps had no idea how long the drug would take to knock out and – with luck – do for Amelia, but she figured on a quarter of an hour or so . . .'

'You believe she intended the stuff should kill Mrs Hatch?' the Vicar enquired dolefully.

Treasure nodded. 'I think so – but she had a secondary plan.'

'Incredible; a sweet old lady like that.' Bantree was shocked.

'I'm afraid if Margaret made up her mind to something, she'd be nothing if not thorough.' Hassock shook his head to emphasize his conviction.

'When Mrs Hatch began to show signs of discomfort, I believe Miss Stopps meant to lead her quickly to the temporary Ladies by the north door . . .'

'Which she did, but she couldn't get in because Witaker had locked himself up there to hide from a ghost.' Bantree was all attention.

'That's where the plan began to go wrong. Miss Stopps needed that room and the SCR to be at her disposal. Hence the call on the house phone earlier – it was intended for Witaker, probably to tell him that Mrs Hatch had been taken ill in some other part of the College.'

'But he'd already left – and Gregory took the call.' Bantree looked quizzical. 'Who was it spoke to Gregory?'

'Miss Stopps herself – the College is littered with telephones. All she had to do was leave Amelia for a few moments when they were near a phone she knew wouldn't be in use. When Gregory answered instead of Witaker she tried to disguise her voice – probably by simply altering the pitch.'

'Hardly ever works,' said Bantree knowingly. 'If you're right, we'll find Gregory will confirm it with the minimum of prompting.' He made another note.

'I believe Miss Stopps intended to leave Amelia to expire, literally locked in a lavatory. But she was first going to bundle the hat, scarf and coat out through the window. After that she needed only to slip outside again and nip into the SCR from the terrace . . .'

'Through the door she'd latched back earlier?' This was Bantree.

Treasure nodded. 'She intended to pick up the bottle and Amelia's glass, and then to join a substitute Mrs Hatch for the fireworks.' Bantree made to interrupt. 'Hang on, Colin – I'll come back to that. The ladies' room is locked, so Miss Stopps takes the only other course open and hurries Amelia into the SCR which she knows is empty. By this time – about ten to six – the victim's down but not out. If she'd been locked in the ladies' room Miss Stopps could have afforded to leave her and still had time to give the drug a chance to take its course. The SCR was another matter. Although the doors could be locked, there were plenty of people with keys.'

'You mean, if she'd been able to use the Ladies, Margaret would have gone in there again after the fireworks to find out if Mrs Hatch was still alive – and if she hadn't been dead then she'd have cut her throat. Oh my God.' Hassock was appalled.

'Something like that, yes – but, as I say, the SCR wasn't nearly so convenient a location for a slow death. Probably Miss Stopps waited a bit, taking Amelia's pulse – that kind of thing. Who knows, it may have appeared she was recovering – and if that was the case, then suicide is just as credible with a knife as it is with drugs.'

'You mean with the Arabian dagger that was conveniently to hand?' There was no emotion in Bantree's tone.

'Almost certainly Miss Stopps took the dagger from Faisal's room when she left the note for Gregory in the room opposite, and after Ribble had treated us to the tour of the royal apartments. She knew we'd been there and she knew the rooms were empty – she probably passed the whole Arab contingent out for their walk as she drove in. Incidentally, Witaker possibly told you he's convinced Amelia pinched the dagger – he swears she was a kleptomaniac.'

Bantree nodded. 'He did imply something of the sort – I thought to get himself off the hook. He's quite keen on the suicide theory still – again for obvious reasons.' The Superintendent paused, and then continued in a matter-of-fact tone. 'Anyway, as you were saying, Miss Stopps got tired of waiting, and cut Mrs Hatch's throat from behind – clean job; no blood on the murderer.'

Hassock sighed: Margaret Stopps had spent half a lifetime keeping blood off her sleeves. 'And the substitute Mrs Hatch?'

'Was Andy, of course – the quite unwitting accomplice.' Treasure watched Bantree's reaction to these words. The policeman nodded slowly. 'Miss Stopps left the SCR with the rum bottle and dirty glass, plus Amelia's outer clothes – they would have been easy enough to remove before Amelia collapsed into the armchair. Andy bears no resemblance to the victim except he's about the right height – but in that long coat, the muffler round his face, and that distinctive hat, he passed muster in the half-light – I'd have sworn he was Amelia.'

'You did,' Bantree observed.

'Andy loves dressing up – Hassock mentioned that to me earlier. The whole charade was a bit of innocent fun for him. As soon as the demonstration began, his instructions were to go into the Hall by the south door and straight out again by the north – he was well ahead of the field. I believe the original plan was for him then to chuck Amelia's things into the ladies' room through the window . . .'

'Which Witaker had thoughtlessly closed to keep out the ghosties.'

'Quite right, Colin. But Miss Stopps was forewarned about that, so Andy's final instructions were to put the hat, coat and scarf into the trunk of the Triumph – possibly the bottle as well. Meantime she got rid of the glass by smashing it during the confusion, and just before she feigned a twisted ankle . . .'

'Ha, which stemmed the flow of people into the Hall.'

'It held some of us up certainly – but Andy had a good start on everybody, and he probably had instructions to go like hell as soon as he was inside.'

'He did, Superintendent.' Hassock spoke quietly. 'I got the whole story out of him before you arrived, from the point where he was to wait for Margaret outside the SCR window – but no one else is going to be told, not by Andy.' He glanced from Bantree to Treasure, and back again. 'It was all a secret game – between Margaret and Andy. Of course he doesn't understand its significance – but so far as he's concerned it's still a secret. I had a devil of a job getting it out of him – and, I repeat, he's not going to spill the beans to anyone else. You see, he'd given his word to Margaret. You'd have to understand their relationship before you could credit what that means to him.'

Bantree looked less uncomfortable at this intelligence than Treasure had expected. 'If Mrs Hatch really had died after the fireworks,' said the policeman, 'in a room she appeared to have locked herself, and with all remotely interested parties accounted for, then assuming the medicos are even marginally wrong about the effects of the drug – the timing, I mean – we could very well have assumed suicide. Circumstantially it could have been an open and shut case.' He gave Treasure what could only be construed as an encouraging glance.

'Goldstein . . .' the banker began tentatively.

'Goldstein,' took up the Superintendent, 'was thoroughly engaged at the real time of the murder making all kinds of inflammatory phone calls from his study. He'd only admit it if we had him on a murder charge, of course, but it would put him in the clear all the same.' He looked sternly at Hassock. 'Vicar, this is a very private conversation – may I rely on your keeping it so?'

'As in the confessional, if you say so, Superintendent.' There was not much demand for the confessional sacrament amongst the Anglicans of Itchendever, but Hassock invested the statement with a gravity that suggested devout queues of penitents. 'I'm not quite clear, though . . .'

'I think I am.' This was Treasure. 'I believe Colin is suggesting he could manage to close this case with the minimum of fuss and hurtful implications for the people and the institutions involved – as well as to the memory of two old ladies who weren't much longer for this world anyway.' He glanced tentatively at Bantree. 'Miss Stopps has paid her penalty. Amelia Hatch's time must have been pretty limited.'

Bantree picked up the letter. 'I believe this was addressed to you, Vicar?' Hassock nodded. The Superintendent passed the two handwritten sheets to the priest. 'Then I don't remember seeing it. Keep it in a safe place for a bit, will you – just in case the coroner's jury encounters any difficulty reaching a verdict of suicide. I don't think it will.' And sure enough, it did not.

Margaret Stopps was sorely missed at Itchendever – both at the College she had done so much to foster and by her adoring grandson who, for a time, was inconsolable. But wounds heal. What remained of Miss Stopps's private fortune – after provision for Andy – proved, after all, to be an insignificant amount. Clearly her resources had not been large enough to cover financial support for both her great loves – a fact that went some way to explain – if not to justify – the desperate course she had adopted.

Through the intervention of Treasure and the wise exercise of the discretion at their command by the new Trustees of the Funny Farms Foundation, not only did UCI receive its half-million dollars, but Andy and Peter Gregory were also included as beneficiaries: each received one-eleventh of the Foundation's capital. As Cyrus Hatch's natural grandson – and his only known direct descendant – Andy, or those acting on his behalf, might well have pressed for a larger sum. In consultation with Mark Treasure it was Marcus Hassock who decided not to pursue this course – in deference to the memory of Miss Stopps and the certainty of what her attitude would have been.

Witaker had no hand in these arrangements. The new and responsible trustees at the Pittsburgh bank sensibly decided on a thorough examining audit of the Foundation's affairs. Although a scandal was averted, Witaker was obliged to make good the shortfall of assets out of his own resources and to resign his position of trust. The fact that all this did not entirely ruin him financially was a measure of greed as unnecessary as it was insatiable.

Eric Ribble and the Crown Prince of Abu B'yat were excused further embarrassing confrontations about a take-over of UCI following the assassination of the Emir in December. Relieved of the need to cultivate the esteem of a father he had not much cared for anyway, the new

Emir graciously accepted an honorary fellowship at the College in return for a generous donation to its Charitable Trust and a tacit understanding that all his sons would be welcome as undergraduates – but not those of his brothers. This arrangement suited him admirably since he did not care for his brothers either, and as Emir he could afford to offend them. It was Daniel Goldstein who actually conferred the fellowship on Sheikh Al Haban in a colourful little ceremony during the Lent term and as an announced contribution to Arab-Jewish understanding – the announcement coming as something of a surprise to the company assembled to hear it, and later described by Goldstein, who had made it, as his pound of flesh.

On his return from Australasia, Lord Grenwood expressed himself well pleased with the situation at UCI. He and Treasure discussed the matter briefly after lunch one day. The Chairman of Grenwood, Phipps was somewhat preoccupied at the time with choosing a new secretary, but on hearing the facts, he did remark that following the suicide of Mrs Hatch and Miss Stopps's sad accident Treasure might well have had a tricky situation on his hands.

Treasure had felt bound to agree.

Also in Hamlyn Paperbacks

David Williams

UNHOLY WRIT

When evidence comes to light that a Shakespeare manuscript is hidden at Mitchell Hall, the Moonlight family's former country seat becomes a centre of death and intrigue.

Merchant banker Mark Treasure is commissioned to buy back the estate, but discovers it has become the headquarters of the fanatical Forward Britain Movement. What is more, an old lady has died of fright and a grave-digger suffered a mysterious and fatal fall.

And linked to these strange incidents are a menacing American posing as a clergyman, a power-hungry MP, and a famous antiquarian supervising a team of Filipino labourers.

Mark Treasure's investigations lead to even more startling revelations – and unexpected rewards.

'By far the best written detective story I have read for months' – Patrick Cosgrave, *Spectator*

'An excellent debut' – *Birmingham Post*

'Lots of characters and plot . . . salted with fun' – *Northern Echo*

A HAMLYN *Whodunnit*

David Williams

COPPER, GOLD & TREASURE

Roderick Copper, retired major, and Benny Gold, London cabbie, apply on the same day for places with the Rudyard Trust for Retired Officers and Gentlemen. But its eccentric and drunken Director tells them the Trust is bankrupt, and its multimillion-pound assets about to be divided among the founder's descendants – a curious, motley crew.

Banker sleuth Mark Treasure is called in when Copper and Gold's bizarre scheme to preserve the charity goes wrong with terrifying consequences – kidnap, stabbing and sudden death.

This ingenious mystery moves rapidly from drama in the Mall to sex in South Kensington, from comedy at Gatwick Airport to tragedy in Victoria – and a gripping finish on the Essex marshes.

'Boisterous farce with grand-slam solution . . . irresistibly comic cast' – Matthew Coady, *Guardian*

'Good old-style detective story . . . briskly told' – H.R.F. Keating, *The Times*

'An eye-opening finale' – John Coleman, *Sunday Times*

A HAMLYN *Whodunnit*

Also in Hamlyn Paperbacks

Peter Dickinson

A PRIDE OF HEROES

There's no murder like a country house murder . . .

. . . and in all the annals of detective fiction, there's never been a country house quite like Herryngs.

Owned by an eccentric baronet . . .

Fabled as the home of 'Old England', Britain's answer to Disneyland . . .

Stalked by man-eating lions and dollar-rich American tourists . . .

Scene of midnight duels on the greensward . . .

Nothing that happens at Herryngs can be described as ordinary – least of all, murder.

A HAMLYN *Whodunnit*

Also in Hamlyn Paperbacks

H.R.F. Keating

INSPECTOR GHOTE DRAWS A LINE

Inspector Ghote is sent to a vast old house in the heat-soaked Indian countryside to investigate threats against the life of Justice Sir Asif Ibrahim, an aged, obstinate and extremely unpopular judge surviving from the British Raj.

The suspects are a motley bunch: Asif's servant, an ex-convict on parole; his jittery spinster daughter whose marriage plans have been thwarted; a rabid left-wing American priest with violent political views; and the local newspaper editor.

Against all odds, Inspector Ghote zealously sifts through numerous false leads – until finally his brilliant inspiration uncovers a monstrous plot.

"Excellent" – **Evening Standard**

"Neatly plotted, tense, with a fast, almost explosive ending" – **Daily Mirror**

"A mixture of wit, gentleness and superb story telling" – **Times of India**

A HAMLYN *Whodunnit*

Also in Hamlyn Paperbacks

Ellery Queen

THE ROMAN HAT MYSTERY

The crime seemed as near perfect as human in-
genuity could make it. When a man is murdered
during a Broadway theatre performance it is found
that his silk hat has vanished. It is there that the
mystery begins – and it continues undiminished
until the final discovery of the murderer. All the
clues are clearly and fairly presented, but it still
takes the utmost skill in juggling with hints and
motives, timetables and personalities to arrive at
the only possible solution.

"If you have a taste for detective tales, read *The
Mystery of the Roman Hat.*" – **J. B. Priestley**.
EVENING NEWS

"One of the best-written, best plotted mystery
yarns." – **EVENING STANDARD**

" ... a worthy successor to Holmes ... At the
end, too, a delectable 'surprise' is not lacking. The
whole thing is most admirably done – the detective
story de luxe." – **SUNDAY TIMES**

A HAMLYN *Whodunnit*

Also in Hamlyn Paperbacks

Jonathan Gash

GOLD FROM GEMINI

Lovejoy, that engaging antique dealer, is temporarily broke and earning a precarious living doing a spot of babysitting.

Then he comes across a series of leads to an apparently mythical 'find' of Roman treasure. His instinct tells him the find is genuine and he'd better unravel the clues.

But before he can do so he is pressed into parting with them in a singularly nasty way ...

Lovejoy's enthusiasm is infectious, and he leaves a trail of murder, mayhem and beautiful ladies in his dangerous hunt for the priceless object that will once and for all make his fortune.

"Decidedly exciting treasure-hunt with Manx climax, some gore and buckets of lore." – **THE TIMES**

"Lovejoy's – and his author's – encyclopedic knowledge of antiques makes his professional expertise entirely convincing." – **FINANCIAL TIMES**

A HAMLYN *Whodunnit*

Also in Hamlyn Paperbacks

Michael Gilbert

BLOOD AND JUDGMENT

One misty November evening a woman's body is found near a reservoir by three boys collecting firewood for Guy Fawkes night. She turns out to be the wife of Monk Ritchie, an escaped criminal – and she has been murdered.

Detective-Sergeant Patrick Petrella has a personal interest in the case, for his colleague still lies unconscious after a beating up by one of Ritchie's gang. Petrella's enthusiasm leads him to working overtime, by night diving in the reservoir.

And though he comes up with a sunken boat, and a body – and the murder weapon – it nearly puts paid to his promising career.

"*Blood and Judgment* must be one of Michael Gilbert's best ... the story combines plausibility with such wickedly clever plotting" – **Stanley Ellin**

A HAMLYN *Whodunnit*

Also in Hamlyn Paperbacks

H.R.F. Keating

THE PERFECT MURDER

It is just Inspector Ghote's luck to be landed with the case of The Perfect Murder at the start of his career with the Bombay Police. For in this baffling crime there's no corpse. Also he has the cunning business tycoon Lala Varde to contend with – and to add to his troubles he finds himself saddled with investigating the mysterious theft of one rupee from the desk of the Minister of Police Affairs and the Arts ...

The Perfect Murder was awarded the Crime Writers Association Golden Dagger and an Edgar Allan Poe Special Award from the Mystery Writers of America.

"How pleasant to meet Mr Ghote! He is one of the most engaging of all fictional detectives." – **Edmund Crispin, Sunday Times**

"Mad, brilliant, touching, ringing fearfully true . . . A book of subtlety and great skill." – **Evening Standard**

A HAMLYN *Whodunnit*

Also in Hamlyn Paperbacks

Michael Gilbert

CLOSE QUARTERS

Anonymous letters, broadsheets, comic flags –
these intrusions on the quiet of Melchester Cathedral Close were sufficient for the Dean to invite his
nephew down from Scotland Yard for a 'holiday'.

Then murder struck – most brutally, and more
than once.

And among the canons and vicars, the vergers,
organist, clerks and constable was one man who
would make that single deadly mistake which has
brought the greatest murderers to the scaffold.

'For murder, though it have no tongue, will speak
with miraculous organ.'

"Mr Michael Gilbert understands the thriller
theory to perfection." – **SPECTATOR**

"Michael Gilbert appeals to that ancient and
simple need in us, the story." – **H. R. F. Keating,**
THE TIMES

"Michael Gilbert is always enjoyable." –
Marghanita Laski, THE LISTENER

A HAMLYN *Whodunnit*